dmlF 1967-68

Young Mr. Football

Other Books by

Marion Renick

BATS AND GLOVES OF GLORY
STEADY, A BASEBALL STORY
DAVID CHEERS THE TEAM
TOMMY CARRIES THE BALL
THE HEART FOR BASEBALL
THE SHINING SHOOTER
THE DOOLEYS PLAY BALL
A TOUCHDOWN FOR DOC
SWIMMING FEVER
SKATING TODAY

For somewhat younger boys and girls

SEVEN SIMPSONS ON SIX BIKES
TODD'S SNOW PATROL
JOHN'S BACK YARD CAMP
JIMMY'S OWN BASKETBALL
PETE'S HOME RUN
NICKY'S FOOTBALL TEAM

Illustrated by

Leonard Shortall

Young Mr. Football

by MARION RENICK

Charles Scribner's Sons   New York

Contents

CHAPTER 1   Bo's Wish   3

2   In Trouble Already   16

3   The Bronze Football   32

4   Katie, the Team Trainer   49

5   The Tackling Dummy   65

6   Mr. Mac's Mystery Coach   78

7   Anything Can Happen in Football   94

8   Bo Spends His Birthday Money   108

9   Another Game, Another Disaster   124

10   The Editor Hears the Story   137

11   Everybody Gets in the Parade   151

12   The Mud Bowl Game   167

13   Hero for a Week   181

14   Rodney's Last Remark   197

Young Mr. Football

Bo's Wish

Bo woke up laughing. First he opened one eye a crack, and saw three chickens, two cows, a brown horse and a red barn. *Where am I?* he thought in a daze. He blinked both eyes and looked again.

All around him were more of the same chickens and cows and brown horse and red barn. Then he started to laugh. The joke was on him. This was the wallpaper in his new room! He and his mother and dad had moved into this house yesterday.

Wide awake now, he sat up to see what else was new to him. The red-covered chair was an old friend of course, but it had changed its place to the other side of his bed. And his work table no longer stood next to the door. It was across the room in front of a window, and—*oh, great!*—outside the window was a big tree.

3

I'll climb that tree, Bo decided at once. Next he thought he would carve his initials on it. Way up high. Higher than anybody ever had climbed before or would climb again. Those initials would remind people of him long after he moved away.

Pleased with his plan, Bo propped his head on the pillows to think about it. Because he and his parents moved from town to town, he no sooner found friends in one place than his father was transferred to another. Bo had made friends from Connecticut to California, yet he had the lonely feeling that they all forgot him when he moved away. He did wish that somewhere the boys and girls would remember him. For this reason he often tried to leave a mark or a record to remind them of him after he left.

Always he had failed.

In the beginning he hoped to do something spectacular, such as setting a record in the fifty-yard dash. On the day of the race, he came in last. Then he dreamed of becoming an outstanding grade-school football player. Since football was his favorite sport, he was sure he could make his mark in it. The trouble was that so few other boys in his school wanted to play the game. That year they were more interested in competing in television speaking contests. He tried this too—and lost all chance of winning when he announced his subject. Due to camera shyness, he sputtered and twisted his words as he always did when he became nervous or excited. "The Dirst Thanksfiving Gay," he said. Although he calmed down and repeated the words slowly and accurately, the judges waved him off the platform.

After that, he tried to leave his mark in simpler ways, once even pressing his hand in fresh-laid cement. This effort, too, came to nothing, for the workmen returned and smoothed out all trace that he had been there.

Now he found himself in a new home with that big tree out there in the front yard. *I'll carve my initials,* he thought again as he looked out into the dark, piny branches. *Better still, I'll carve my whole name.* He tried to imagine HAROLD BOWLING slashed into the rough bark. Nobody who saw that would forget him.

From outside came a single thump which made him leap to the window. "Golly day, somebody's kicking a football!" he said aloud. In the street below he saw a boy about his own age who was shouting, "Hurry up, Katie!" Half way down the block was a girl running after the ball. She caught it and threw it back to the boy. Again came the sound which had thrilled Bo—the *plunk* of a football kicked straight and hard. He did not wait to see how far the ball went. He snatched his shirt and jeans from the

5

red chair. In two zips and a wiggle he was dressed and on his way downstairs, carrying his shoes. The lock on the unfamiliar front door stopped him for a moment, then he was outdoors on the steps just in time to see Katie return the ball. It fell short and came bobbing end over end almost to his bare feet.

A door slammed at the next house and a small boy shot across the lawn shouting, "What you *doo-oo*-ing?" Then, seeing the grounded ball, he pranced toward it like a puppy after a stick. "I'll get it! I'll get it for you, Barry!"

Bo was already bending over the ball. Here was his chance to show he knew how to handle it. He remembered what he had learned from his father, who had been a football player himself. He lifted the ball to his ear, got on balance with his forward foot pointing to the boy in the street, drew back his arm and let fly.

The small boy beside him followed the ball with his eyes, saying, "That's pretty good for playing football with your shoes off."

Both older boys laughed. The one called Barry said to the youngster, "You don't need shoes on to throw the ball, Tyler." He added with a nod of approval at Bo, "That pass of yours was all right."

"Your kick was a good one too," Bo said. "I watched you from my window. Golly day! You have power."

6

"Do you really think so?" Barry seemed pleased and came toward him, holding the ball in an easy way as if he were quite accustomed to carrying it. Bo was dying to know if he played on a football team. "I say, do you flay on a pootball team?" he blurted, forgetting how his tongue always betrayed him in moments of excitement.

Barry must not have noticed the odd words. Either that, or he was one of those excellent fellows who never calls attention to your mistakes. He answered, "Not a regular team. We have only a sort of one."

Bo grew even more excited. If there was no regular team, perhaps he would have a chance to play! He took great care not to twist his words this time as he asked, "Is it a school team?"

The girl now came across the lawn. Bo knew at once she was Barry's sister. Their faces were alike and they both had the same round brown eyes, except that hers were more serious than Barry's. It was she who answered Bo's question. "Oh, Cedarville Elementary School doesn't have a football team."

"But some of us play in the schoolyard at recess, Katie. You know we do," her brother said. Turning to Bo he explained, "The only football field in town is at the high school. So only high school boys can have real teams. Here in this neighborhood, we play in the street because it's a dead end and pretty safe. But as I said, we have only a sort of a team."

"Yes, we told you," young Tyler echoed. "Only a sort of a team."

Even this, Bo thought, promised more football than any other neighborhood he had lived in. He was about to ask more questions when a woman opened the door of the pale yellow house across the street. "Katie! Barry!" she called. "Breakfast!"

"We're coming!" brother and sister answered together. As they started away Barry held up the football in his hand as a sort of signal to Bo. "I'll see you later."

"We're going to the city right after breakfast," Katie told Bo. "We're going shopping, and to pick up Daddy at his office. Then we'll have lunch at the Purple Cow."

"You ought to eat there sometime," Barry yelled to Bo from across the street. "They have twenty-seven kinds of ice cream."

"Yes, *sir*. Twenty-seven kinds of ice cream," Tyler repeated to Bo. "What do you think of that?"

"That's more kinds than you could eat at one time." Bo gave him a smile which set the small boy dancing with happiness until, in a final burst of joy, he stood on his head. Viewing Bo upside down he said, "I saw you move into this house yesterday."

8

Back on his feet again he asked, "Did you know you were going to live next door to me? . . . What's your name? . . . Do you like to build tunnels with blocks?" He popped questions like beans out of a shooter until he, too, was called home to breakfast.

Bo put on his shoes and went indoors, calling upstairs, "Hey, Mom! Dad! Get up! This is a good place. We're going to like it here. The kids play football. There's a boy right across the street, and twenty-seven kinds of ice cream at the Curple Pow, and—"

"We're up already!" Mother called from the kitchen. Bo followed her voice as she added, "Daddy heard you open the front door and it made him think of breakfast."

Yesterday, Bo remembered, after the moving van drove away, he and his parents went hunting for a place to eat dinner and buy milk, bread and eggs for this morning. Now as he came into the kitchen, Mother was scrambling those eggs in her favorite iron skillet. The battered coffee pot was gurgling on its accustomed burner at the back of the same old stove. Three blue plates, cups and saucers welcomed him as usual from the well-known yellow table where Dad, with his ear to the toaster, now reported, "It survived another moving. It's beginning to tick."

In one of the unfamiliar cupboards Bo found his pet glass, which said ROSE BOWL, PASADENA, CALIFORNIA on it. He filled it with milk and carried it to the table. The Bowlings sat down to breakfast as though they had lived in this house all their lives.

"How nice to have a big kitchen with our table by a window," Mother said.

"Didn't I just tell you this is a good place?" Bo bounced in his chair, eager to start exploring. He wanted to find those other boys on the street who played football. Also there was the big tree out in front to be climbed.

First of all, though, Dad asked Mother, "What can Harold and I do to help us get settled?"

"The books have to be unpacked and put on the shelves," she said. "That's a good job for you, Harold. Daddy and I can hang the pictures and put up the curtains."

By noon the house began to look like home. Mother said it was time to stop work, have a bite to eat and make themselves presentable. "Lila Sanders and her husband are apt to drop in, and I'd hate to have them find us so dirty we couldn't even shake hands."

Bo had heard about Lila Sanders all his life. She and Mother had been girlhood friends. "And now Lila has a little boy just the same age as you," Mother was always telling him, even though he had stopped being little a long time ago.

"What makes you think she'll come today?" Dad asked.

"Oh, I have a hunch," Mother said. "I discovered that Mifflin, where they live, is a twin suburb to this one. The two villages are side by side. So I sent Lila this address and the date we expected to move in. She wrote back that they would drop around to welcome us. That is so like her. Lila always was the dearest, friendliest girl. I do hope she brings her little boy Rodney. He's the same age as you, Harold, and it will be so nice for you two to get acquainted."

"Mmmm," Bo said, thinking his own thoughts.

A few minutes later he was pulling on a clean shirt when he heard a car stop in front of the house. He looked out and whistled to himself. "Whee-ee! Look at the size of that! Pretty sharp!"

A man and a woman unfolded themselves from the shiny black car, followed by a rather large boy. Bo, who was thinner but perhaps more muscular, figured he could hold his own against this newcomer. Bounding downstairs he was presented to "Aunt Lila" and "Uncle Harry." Then someone said, "And this is Rodney."

Bo found himself looking straight into pale blue eyes which stared at him with no interest whatsoever, as if he were invisible. He fought against this uncomfortable feeling by staring back at Rodney's chubby pink cheeks and wavy brown hair. The deadlock was broken when Mrs. Bowling said, "While we grownups are talking, Harold, why don't you and Rodney have a gingerale in the kitchen?"

Even this pleasant suggestion caused no flicker of interest in Rodney's pale eyes, Bo noticed as he turned to lead the way to the kitchen. He thought the other boy didn't want to follow, but when he opened the refrigerator door, there was Rodney right at his elbow, peering in and remarking, "Gee, don't you have anything in here to eat? We keep ours full. Any time I want it, there's cold chicken and oranges and salami—four or five kinds of salami—" He broke off as Bo lifted out a bottle of gingerale. Then— "You don't expect to drink that stuff plain, do you? We always put ice cream in gingerale at our house."

"We haven't been here long enough to buy ice cream," Bo said cheerfully. "We just moved in yesterday afternoon. We wouldn't even have any gingerale if we hadn't brought this with us from Pasadena." He began to hunt for a bottle opener, looking into this drawer and that, muttering, "Where did Mom put it *this* time?"

Rodney said, "At our house we never have to hunt for an opener. We have a thing fastened on the wall."

"That would be handy," Bo agreed. Having found the

opener, he now was pouring the gingerale into two glasses. He handed one to his guest who took it without a thank-you, sipped, and said, "This needs ice."

Bo explained they had forgotten to fill the ice trays until about an hour ago.

"And you don't have ice yet?" Rodney raised his eyebrows. "Your refrigerator must be a hundred years old. We have the newest model. It makes ice cubes as fast as we can fill the trays."

"That would be handy," Bo repeated. He was wondering what to do with Rodney when their glasses were empty. He need not have worried. Rodney began amusing himself by opening cupboard doors and looking in. Evidently finding nothing worthy of his interest, he started toward the back door. "Let's go out to the patio. At our house, that's where we always—oh, I see you don't have one. I'd certainly hate to live in a house which doesn't have a patio."

Only good manners kept Bo from saying nobody had asked Rodney to live here. By this time they were out of doors, walking around the house. Even Rodney was impressed with the tree in front. "I'll bet that's a good one to climb," he said.

This praise made Bo feel so friendly toward him for the moment that he confided, "Someday I'm going to carve

14

my initials way up high on the trunk—higher than anybody else can climb it."

"You think you'll set some kind of record, eh?" Rodney
only stared at him. "What for? Any record you'd set in
Cedarville wouldn't be worth peanuts. It would be forgotten the next day."

CHAPTER TWO

In Trouble Already

Bo was sorry he had mentioned climbing the tree. Perhaps carving his initials wasn't a very important way of making an unforgettable name for himself, but he had failed at so many other ways that this was about the only one left. Now Rodney was sneering at it. And belittling his new home town too.

"What's wrong with Cedarville?" Bo asked, beginning to grow angry.

"It's a dead hole. Everybody knows that." Rodney shrugged. "You ought to live in Mifflin, where I do. Boy, there's more going on there in ten minutes than there is here in ten years."

"Like what?" Bo knew this reply was weak, but it was the best he could think of at the moment.

"Like right now," Rodney said with triumph. "What are we doing but standing here? In Mifflin there would be lots of fellows around and we'd be playing games. At my house I have a big wooden chest full of all kinds of games. Parchesi, chess, Monopoly—"

"We could play checkers," Bo suggested.

"That baby game? I haven't played checkers since I was in the first grade. Chess is my game. Chess for indoors and football for outdoors. My football coach says—"

"Football!" Bo almost gave a cheer. At last he knew how to entertain Rodney. "Wait till I get mine. We can kick it around in the street."

His playthings weren't unpacked yet, so he had to spend some time hunting his football. When he brought it out, Rodney at once took it into his own hands. "It's too soft," he said as he flipped it into the air. "I always keep my footballs—both of them—well inflated."

Rodney certainly knew how to pass, Bo admitted to himself. A boy who could do that well with a spongy ball couldn't be such a complete stinker as he seemed. However, after retrieving twelve or fifteen long passes, Bo went back to his first opinion about Rodney—especially when Rodney said he supposed Bo was learning a lot of football from watching a specialist in passing.

Bo, who was also interested in other departments of

football, was still hoping for a chance to tackle and block, when he heard a door slam at the next house. Then a squeaky shout, "What you *doo-oo*-ing?"

Young Tyler came rocketing across the lawn after the ball. "I'll get it! Let *me* get it!" Bo was glad to let him.

Returning with the ball, Tyler gave it to Bo although Rodney held out his hands for it and promptly snatched it. Tyler gave him a long look. "Who is *he?*" he asked Bo. "Did he move here with you?"

Bo shook his head. Tyler said, "That's good. We don't need him." Off he ran to retrieve the pass Rodney threw. Once more he returned the ball to Bo. Rodney said Tyler was interfering and told him to go home.

"Oh, skip it, Rodney," said Bo. "He isn't hurting any-thing. Let him stay." To keep peace—and also because he wanted to play a little football himself—he suggested to his guest, "Why don't we practice tackling for a while?"

Rodney's eyebrows went up. "What for? I always carry the ball, or else pass it. My coach says I don't need to tackle."

"Tackling is important too." Bo was going to add that his father said so and his father had been a football player. But Rodney asked first, "How many games have *you* played in?"

By this time Bo was so angry his tongue betrayed him into sputtering, "Haybe I 'aven't played in many—"

It was saying "many" when he meant "any" that started all the trouble for him—trouble in which, before the end came, dozens of people took sides and the honor of Cedarville had to be decided. He could not foresee this of course. When he realized he had twisted his words he only bit his tongue. It was too late to correct himself, to say, "Maybe I haven't played in any—"

The instant Rodney heard the word "many" he snapped, "I'll bet you haven't played in as many games as I have. I'm the star ball-carrier on our team. I'd like to play against you in a game and show you some real playing. But I suppose—" he raised his eyebrows at the houses round about, "—I suppose the fellows here don't know a scrimmage from a goal post. I feel sorry for you, moving into a place like Cedarville where the boys don't even play football."

"We do too play football," Tyler said. He looked at Bo. "Don't we?"

Bo spoke one careful word. "Yes."

Rodney stared right through both of them as he asked in a bored way, "If the boys here have a team, why hasn't it been mentioned in the *Two-Village Weekly Times?*

You can read all about *my* team in that newspaper. We've been trying to get a game with Cedarville. The *Times* has run our challenge. If your crew can play, then why don't they answer us?" Rodney shrugged. "Afraid to, I suppose."

"We're not afraid!" Tyler shouted at Rodney then turned to Bo. "Tell him! You tell him. We aren't afraid to play his old team, are we?"

"Dolly gay, I sould shay not!" There Bo did it again! He quickly tried to correct himself and say, "Golly day, I should say not!" But before he could take a calm breath Rodney was hooting, "Dolly Gay? Who's she—your girl friend?"

Bo ground his teeth as Rodney went on, "How did she get into this? It sounds to me like you're trying to back out of playing us. Will you or won't you? Say yes or no."

Tyler gave a big shout, "YES!" Rodney seemed to think Bo had joined in it for he stared in his direction and said with a perfectly blank face, "Good. We'll show you a thing or two about setting records." He then stood as if awaiting some comment from Bo.

Bo kept still. He didn't know what to say. Here was Rodney expecting a game with "his" team. He didn't want to admit Cedarville had no team, nor did he want to throw the blame on little Tyler for speaking out in matters which concerned older boys. Besides, if he did *that* Rodney would never let him live it down. *Maybe he'll forget about the game if I don't say anything more,* was Bo's hopeful thought.

Rodney seemed disappointed by Bo's silence. His parting shot as he left with his parents was, "Let me know when you set a record—so I can beat it." This plainly was intended to sting Bo into making a reply. Bo did reply, in his own way. He laughed to himself, "The joke will be on him when I make a mark he can't even touch." Then turning back to the house he took a long look at the big tree. Climbing it would call for strength and endurance and nerve. Furthermore he would have to carve his whole name up there, he decided. Initials were not enough for the kind of record he intended to set. Even as he made this decision, Rodney's words sneaked into his mind and stole the glory from his project. *Any record you'd set in Cedarville wouldn't be worth peanuts. It would be forgotten the next day.*

At that moment Mrs. Bowling said briskly, "Lila told me there is a shopping center at the other end of this street. Suppose we all go and lay in some food for the week end."

"I'm heartily in favor of that," Dad said. "While you buy groceries, Bo and I will scout around for a drugstore, and get an evening paper."

Shortly afterward Bo was walking along the main street of Cedarville. "Look!" He jogged his father's arm. "There is the place where we ate last night. *Shingledecker's.*" He chuckled as he repeated the name on the restaurant window. Odd-sounding names always amused him. He began to look for others on the signs over the shops here in his new home town. Ahead a few steps was *Muzzey's Laundromat.* That wasn't so odd perhaps, but how about the one beyond it? *A. Squeeo, Plumber.* He was so delighted with *Weatherwax and Sons* across the street he almost missed the red neon loops which spelled *Ryan's Pharmacy.*

"Here's a drugstore," Dad said. In they went, to be greeted by a short, bald-headed man boxed from neck to knees in a stiff white coat. Across the pocket of the coat a name was stitched in small red letters: *Tom Ryan.*

While Dad bought his paper, Bo looked around the store. At once his attention was caught by a bronze football resting on a base of black wood at one end of the counter. He reached out to touch the metal laces and feel the seams, which were like those of a real football. Then he noticed several names engraved on the smooth side of the ball. The first of them was *Scott Freeman.* Bo was sure he had heard that name before. He was trying to remember where, when Mr. Ryan called out to him, "That's our Cedarville Football Trophy."

Both the druggist and Mr. Bowling came to look at the trophy with Bo. As soon as Dad saw the names on it, he asked Mr. Ryan, "Is that the same Scott Freeman who played in the Rose Bowl last New Year's Day?"

"The very same," Tom Ryan answered, looking proud.

Dad turned to Bo. "You remember him, don't you?"

Bo certainly did! "We lived in Pasadena then," he explained to the druggist. "We went to the big game and the crowd yelled 'Scotty!' so hard Mother put her hands over her ears. Dad told me never to forget I had just seen Scott Freeman win the Rose Bowl Game." As Bo finished, he looked with more interest than ever at the bronze football. He asked, "Is his name on this because he won that game?"

"No, no." The druggist looked surprised. "Don't you know? He was born here and grew up here. I thought everybody knew that. Yes, sir, Cedarville is the home of the great Scott Freeman, except for the time he is away at State U. of course."

"Maybe you'll see him on the street someday. Or in this drugstore," Dad said to Bo with a glance at Mr. Ryan, who nodded.

"Really?" Bo at once looked at the other customers in the store, half expecting one of them to be wearing a football uniform.

24

"If you want to see Scotty," the druggist said, "come down to the old recreation park tomorrow afternoon at three o'clock. The Boosters Club has made arrangements for him to give a football demonstration for the kids of the community." He turned to Mr. Bowling. "That's why the trophy is here just now. I brought it over from the library next door, where it is kept on display. I want to shine it up before I take it to the jamboree tomorrow. We'd like to show the boys the honor they can win if they try hard enough."

"You mean a boy can win this?" Bo touched the bronze ball.

"That's what it's for," Tom Ryan said. "A boy doesn't get to take it home of course. Better than that, his name is engraved upon it and the trophy is kept where everybody can see it and remember the record he made."

Bo's heart thumped. *Here was the place to carve his name. Not on a tree but on this trophy where—Mr. Ryan said so!—everybody would remember him.* Breathless with excitement he could feel a dozen questions tumbling on his tongue. He allowed himself only one untwistable word. "How?"

"Read what it says on that metal plate on the base," the druggist told him.

Bo read the words to himself. Dad read them aloud.

THE CEDARVILLE TROPHY
AWARDED ANNUALLY BY THE BOOSTERS CLUB
TO THE BOY WHO BEST CARRIES ON OUR
FOOTBALL TRADITION

"As you see, Scotty was the first to be awarded this trophy," Mr. Ryan said, pointing to the engraved names. "We Boosters started it because of him. We wanted to encourage other youngsters to live up to the fine example of clean fun, hearty competition and fair play set by Scott Freeman."

"I suppose only high school boys are eligible to compete for the trophy." Dad spoke the very thought in Bo's mind.

"No, no. There is no age limit. True, all the boys who have won the honor were in high school at the time. High school boys naturally have more opportunity to distinguish themselves in games. But there is no reason why youngsters this age—" Mr. Ryan patted Bo's shoulder, "—can't try for it. We believe in starting 'em out right, here in Cedarville."

"An excellent idea," Mr. Bowling agreed.

"Then you'd better join us Boosters. Yes, sir." Mr. Ryan held out his hand. "I'm Tom Ryan, and your name is—"

"Bowling. Hal Bowling. And this is my son, Harold."

"They call me Bo, though," Bo said as Mr. Ryan shook hands all around.

"You're newcomers, I judge. We are always glad to welcome—" Mr. Ryan was saying as Bo turned back to the football trophy to read again: *awarded . . . to the boy who best carries on our Football Tradition.* "Wait till I tell old Rodney about this," he said to himself. Rodney had claimed Cedarville was a poor place for football and that the boys here knew nothing about the game. This would show him!

Dad was leaving the store now. As Bo followed, Mr. Ryan took time from a customer to remind him, "I'll look for you with the rest of the kids tomorrow. Three o'clock at the old recreation park. Go to the bridge at the foot of this street and turn left along the river. There's nothing there any more except the old shelter house. That's where we'll meet. Don't forget."

"I sure won't," Bo said. He wondered if the boy across the street knew about the meeting. Maybe they could go together. All the way home he thought how much fun that would be. He sat on the front step and watched for Barry and his sister to return from the city, wondering if they would be as friendly as they had been in the morning. He need not have wondered. About a minute after their car turned into their drive, Barry came across the street followed by Katie. They had the football. "Want to kick it around with us?" Barry asked.

After they had played a while they sat on the curb and talked. Bo discovered he and Katie were the same age although he was a grade behind her. This was the result of his having changed schools so often. He was glad he had lost a year because it meant he now would be in the same class with Barry.

"You'll have somebody to tell you what your homework is," Katie said to her brother. She explained to Bo with a little shake of her short black curls, "He forgets things. It's a wonder sometimes he doesn't forget his own name."

Barry's eyes twinkled. "Don't believe everything she says."

Bo had a sudden thought. "By the way, what *is* your name? Your last name, I mean."

"Hunt." Barry and Katie spoke at once. "What's yours?"

"Bowling. Bo for short."

"Bowling?" Brother and sister smiled at each other. "Bowling?" Barry asked again, making a sweep with one arm as if to send a ball rolling along an alley to knock over the wooden pins.

Bo had to chuckle. All his life he had been amused by odd names. Never once had he thought his own name might seem odd to other people. Barry and Katie laughed, too, in a friendly way which made Bo think how much better he liked this boy than Rodney. Remembering Rodney started him to wondering if he should tell Barry he had by mistake let Rodney get the idea the Cedarville boys were willing to accept the challenge of the Mifflin football team. On second thought, he decided Rodney probably would forget the whole deal. Besides, Bo was more interested at the moment in finding out if Barry knew about Scott Freeman and the Boosters Club football jamboree the next afternoon.

"Sure," Barry said when Bo asked.

Katie added, "It's for girls too. We're going, aren't we, Barry?"

Barry nodded and said to Bo, "Why don't you come?"

From then on the talk was all about the bronze football trophy and what a boy would have to do to get his name on it. Barry was impressed when Bo told about seeing Scott Freeman play in the Rose Bowl. Bo was impressed when the Hunts told of meeting Scotty in Ryan's drugstore when he was home from college. Bo asked about the Boosters Club. "It's a bunch of businessmen here in Cedarville," Katie said. "Daddy belongs to it but he hardly ever goes to the meetings because his office is in the city. He's a lawyer."

"My dad sells machines that add and subtract and multiply and work out problems," Bo explained in turn. "He doesn't have any office, except the main one in Pittsburgh. That's why we move around so much. The main office sends him to different places to sell these machines."

"Does he let you do your math on them?" Barry asked. They all laughed over the thought of doing homework by pushing buttons.

Soon a long whistle was heard from the Hunts' side of the street. "That's Dad calling us for dinner," said Katie.

When they left, Bo hurried to report to his mother and father that Cedarville was really the best place they ever had lived, and that they needn't make any plans for him for the next afternoon because he was going with some friends to the football demonstration.

"We are invited to the Sanders' for supper," Mother reminded him. "I thought you would want to go early and play with Rodney."

"I'll have plenty of time to play with him." Bo did not mean this in the pleasant way his mother seemed to take it, but he did not correct her.

"Good," she said. "I'll call Lila and tell her what time we'll be there. You can talk to Rodney too."

Bo would rather have talked to anyone else in the world,

but his mother handed him the phone so he had to say, "Hello."

Rodney's first words, drawled over the wire, gave him a sinking feeling. "Everything is all set for that game you promised us. My team says we'll play Cedarville any Saturday you choose, provided it's early in October."

"Ugp," Bo gulped.

"Of course we don't expect much of a contest," Rodney continued. "It will help *your* team, though, to see how football is really played and how somebody like me handles the ball."

Bo had been hoping Rodney would forget his mixed-up words of that afternoon about playing football. Fearful of what he had started, he began to stutter, "We—I—"

"Wee eye," Rodney repeated. "There you go talking nonsense. Why don't you say what you mean?"

The harder Bo tried, the more twisted his words became. "The Cevardille cleam tan't pay you."

"Baby talk." Rodney's laugh was low and unpleasant. "You'll look like babies, all of you, by the time my team gets through with you."

CHAPTER THREE

The Bronze Football

So much happened to Bo on his first day in Cedarville that the next morning he could hardly believe it was only the second time he had awakened in the room with the chickens, cows, horses and red barns. He felt as if he had lived here for years.

Looking out the window, he smiled to himself at the thought of his childish plan to carve his initials on the big tree. Today he had an older boy's ambition to engrave his name among the football heroes of the town.

He wadded a pillow under his head and lay thinking about the bronze football trophy. He could plainly see that to win it he would have to make a start by playing football games. Well, he already had a game arranged, didn't he? Thanks to Rodney for pushing him into it. *Good old Rodney,* Bo laughed. *He did me a favor although I didn't realize it till now.*

The next thing Bo had to do was get a team together. But how? For all he knew, Barry and his friends might not even want to play a regular game. If they did, they certainly would have answered the Mifflin team's challenge themselves, wouldn't they?

Another question: How would they feel about a newcomer who had taken up that challenge for them without even telling them beforehand? He thought they might be so sore they wouldn't play with him at all. What would he do then?

He decided these questions were too much for him to settle before breakfast. He put them out of his mind until later. When he did start to think about them again, Dad interrupted, "How about running down to Tom Ryan's drugstore and getting the Sunday papers, son? Think you can find the way?"

Bo hurried off, happy to have another look at the bronze football. It was not in sight when he entered the drugstore. He didn't see Mr. Ryan either. "Tom took the trophy with him," said the clerk in answer to Bo's questions. "He's going to display it at some football meeting that's going to be held today in the old recreation park. He might even be on his way there now."

This news was enough to send Bo to the same place, weighed down though he was by a thick stack of newspapers. He remembered the druggist's directions—down the street to the bridge, then turn right. He found himself in a vast field of weeds a-buzz with crickets and jumping with grasshoppers. There was one single tree—*even bigger than the one in our yard,* he thought. It did its best to make a spot of shade with the help of a weather-beaten shelter house. Beneath the sagging roof were a few wobbly benches and an old picnic table upon which someone was sitting. Expecting to see Mr. Ryan, Bo pushed forward through the weeds. When he stepped out of the bright sunlight onto the cracked cement floor, he found not the druggist but a red-haired young man wearing a white T shirt over a pair of powerful, sunburned shoulders. This fascinating person was nibbling the tender end of a long blade of grass which bobbed up and down as he said, "Hi, boy!"

"Hi," said Bo. Then, because he was looking for it and didn't see it, he asked, "Do you know where the bronze football is?"

The young man looked puzzled. Bo explained, "The football trophy with Scott Freeman's name on it."

The stranger shook his head. Seeing Bo's disappointment, he added, "I am Scott Freeman, though. If that will be of any help to you."

Bo was so excited he almost cried out, "Are you really

Frott Sceeman?" He held onto himself, took a long breath and said slowly, "You are! Honestly?"

The redhead nodded. There was a long silence. Then Bo said, looking up at those strong shoulders, "I saw you win the Rose Bowl Game last New Year's Day."

"I didn't win it." The blade of grass bobbed again. "There were ten other men on our team who had as much to do with our victory as I did."

Bo thought this over in another long silence. He looked up again. Golly day, what powerful shoulders! What strong arms and big hands! He said, "I'll bet you can shove a tackler right out of your way when you're headed for the goal line."

Scott Freeman laughed. His teeth were white and strong-looking too, Bo noticed. "I've stiff-armed many a tackle," he said. "So has every other ball carrier."

This time the silence was shorter. Bo boosted himself onto the table beside Scott and said, "I'm coming back to hear you talk about football this afternoon."

"Good. I'm glad somebody is coming," the football star said. "There's a whole truckload of bleachers on the way out here from the high school gym. We borrowed them for this afternoon, and I've been sitting here waiting to help set them up and wondering if any kids will come to sit on them."

"My friend Barry is coming too," Bo said, trying to sound encouraging. He thought of saying he would bring Tyler too, but decided against it. Tyler was too young to appreciate the fine points of football. He finished, "And Barry's sister is coming with us."

"Good!" Scott said again. "That makes three, anyway. Better bring your own sisters and brothers too."

"I don't have any," Bo said, then corrected himself. "I mean I don't *think* I have any."

"Don't you know for sure?" Scott stared at him in amazement.

Bo didn't want Scott to think him so stupid he didn't even know who was in his own family. So he explained something he never mentioned to anyone and seldom even thought about. "I'm—I'm adopted. I've been with Mother and Dad since I was a little tiny baby. *We* don't have any other boys or girls . . . But I may have some brothers and sisters somewhere. You know how it is," he ended in a low voice.

"Indeed I do know how it is," Scott threw away the long tail of grass and said with a quiet smile, "I am adopted too."

"Oh!" Bo thought this was the most wonderful thing that ever had happened to him. A strong brown arm went around his shoulders as a big brother's would do. He wanted to wriggle closer, but sat very straight and laid one hand on Scott's knee instead. "I've never known anybody before who was—like us."

"There are lots of us." Scott gave him a pat. "We are all mighty lucky. Mighty lucky! We have wonderful parents—"

"We sure do!" said Bo. "I'm going right home and tell mine about you. It is kind of like—" he chuckled happily, "—like finding a brother."

"Indeed it is." Scott nodded. "And if I can ever help my kind-of-like younger brother, you just call on me. My family are the only Freemans in the Cedarville phone book. You can find our number easily."

In return Bo promised with his whole heart, "If I can ever help *you,* I'll do *anything.*"

"Thanks, old man. I hope you'll start this afternoon by bringing all your friends. And tell them to ask questions. We need kids to speak up when I call for questions at the end of my talk."

"What kind of questions?"

"Any kind you want to ask about football," Scotty said. "For example, do *you* have any questions about football which are troubling you?"

"Do I? Golly day, I have a couple of whoppers!" Bo drew a happy sigh. Here was somebody who might help solve the problems his excitable tongue had got him into. Although he had been too proud to admit this weakness to Rodney Sanders, or even to Barry, he did not mind telling his whole story to Scott Freeman. The only thing he kept to himself was his secret longing to win a place for his name on the bronze football. "What shall I do?" he asked when he finished. "Barry said the Cedarville boys don't even have a team."

"Don't they play football at all?" Scotty seemed disappointed.

"Oh, they have a sort of a team, he says. Eight or ten fellows kicking and passing in the street. That's all."

"Will those boys be here this afternoon?"

"I suppose so." Bo nodded.

"Then your troubles are over!" Scotty thumped him on the back. "All we need do is get them so steamed up about football they can't wait to organize a team that will show Mifflin who's the champion of the two villages."

"Hooray!" Bo shouted, spilling the newspapers which he had held under his arm all this time. As he picked them up he asked, "Do you really think we can do it?"

"Leave it to me," Scotty said. "Just you make sure those boys get here, and I'll—" before he could finish, a small truck came rattling into the field and pulled at the sagging shelter house. Scotty went to help the men unload. Bo

38

started for home with the newspapers. As he looked back for a last glimpse of his hero, Scott waved to him with a cheery, "See you later!"

In a few hours Bo was back again with Barry and Katie. The bleachers were up and groups of youngsters already were trying them to see which seats were best. Druggist Tom Ryan and the bronze football trophy were to be seen on a platform made of long picnic tables pushed together. Scott Freeman also was on the platform with several younger fellows. "High school players," Barry reported. They all wore football uniforms.

"Here's room for the three of us," Barry said, settling on the first empty bench they came to—one of the farthest from the platform.

"Let's find seats up in front," said Bo. He hadn't told his friends about his earlier visit to this place. That conversation with Scott he felt was a secret between him and the football player. But now he wanted to make sure Scott knew he was here. Bo hoped to signal him that Cedarville's "sort of" players were present, ready to be turned into a real team.

The bleachers filled rapidly with bouncing, squealing, squirming, shouting boys, with a few girls scattered about. Tom Ryan quieted them somewhat by calling the meeting to order. He introduced Scott Freeman amid thunderous cheers, which died out immediately because nobody wanted to miss a word spoken by the All-American back and Cedarville's most famous citizen.

Scotty stood for a moment, smiling down at them. He said he was impressed by the large amount of football muscle gathered there in front of him. "I hope I can help you make the best use of what each of you has," he said. "If you want to be an athlete, the first thing to learn is to take care of your body. Think how much care is given to an airplane. Well, your body is much more valuable than even a million-dollar plane. A pilot wouldn't think of taking off unless he first warmed up his engine, would he?"

"No! No!" the boys shouted.

"Okay. Don't you take off either—or start to play football—without first warming up your muscles. Doing this is one way to avoid injuries. Another way is to build up your muscles till they're so strong that hard knocks won't hurt you."

Scotty stepped to the edge of the platform and looked from boy to boy as he asked, "How many of you want to have a hard, healthy body, like an athlete?"

Shouts came from all over. "I do! I do, Scotty!" Bo felt a thrill shoot through him. He was sure the football player gave him a little nod as he, too, raised his hand with an "I do!"

40

"Good!" Scotty spread out his arms as if he would have hugged the whole bunch. "All you need is to eat properly and get plenty of exercise. Drink lots of milk and eat lots of vegetables, especially the colored ones—green lettuce and spinach; yellow carrots; red beets. And go easy on the sweet stuff. Cake and pie and candy and pop do not build muscles. What's worse, they'll take away your appetite for the foods that do make you strong.

"The other thing to remember is to keep your muscles working. If you sit and watch television too much, or if you ride everywhere you go, your muscles will get lazy. Lazy muscles are weak and soft. Remember *that* the next time you want your parents to drive you to school or over your paper route. *Walk* wherever you possibly can. Also, do exercises like these."

Scotty raised his arms sideways, held them shoulder high and moved them in small circles. "Rotate them gently, like this. First forward, then backward," he said. "This exercise builds strength and endurance . . . Here's another that does too: Lie on your back. Raise first one leg, then the other. Do that ten times. Then raise both legs together, ten times."

Another exercise he called the Jumping Jack. With a little hop, he spread his feet apart and swung his arms up sideways until his hands clapped together above his head.

With a second hop, he brought his feet together again and swung his hands down to his sides. "There's swell rhythm in this one," he said, counting. "One, two. Clap, down. Clap, down." He stopped jumping and went on to say, "All these exercises help prevent injuries. Do them every day. Use them to loosen your muscles before a game. And remember, once your muscles are warm, don't get chilled. You've seen football players sitting on the bench wearing heavy jackets, haven't you? Well, they are taking care to keep their bodies from cooling off too quickly."

Bo remembered how his mother and dad always stopped him from peeling off his shirt when he came into the house, all hot from running. He often thought they were too fussy about this. Now he understood. Dad knew how to take care because he had played football himself. He would also agree with Scotty's statement, "Young players should wear helmets for protection, and shoulder and hip pads, too, if possible."

"Now, you linemen—" Scotty was saying as he crouched, feet slightly apart and one hand resting on the ground in front of him. "This is your stance, when the teams line up. We call it the three-point position. Some of your weight is on this forward hand. You are ready and cocked to spring forward at the man across from you. See?" He came out of his stance and darted ahead so fast he couldn't stop himself when he came to the edge of the platform. He had to jump off, which made the youngsters laugh. He climbed back, laughing, too, and saying, "If you're playing in the backfield, you crouch without leaning on your hand. A back must be ready to move to either side as well as straight ahead."

Scotty came out of his backfield stance with a quick lunge to the right. "See what I mean?" he asked them. Then he stood up and said with great seriousness. "If you can take off in a hurry—and run fast—you can play football. Football is a game of legs."

Then he showed the boys how to run. "Be a power runner," he told them. "Lean forward. Get that high knee action. Use your arms to propel yourself. Push *straight* ahead. Run on your toes. That makes your legs longer and you can go faster and drive harder."

Bo drank in every word. There was so much to learn. Every now and then he and Barry gave each other a look which said, "We must remember *this*."

Others, too, seemed to feel everything Scotty said was important to them. There wasn't a fidget or a whisper— not even from the girls. When Scotty stopped to ask, "Have you had enough? Or shall I go on?" a roar came from his audience. "More! More! Please, more!"

He laughed and shook his head saying, "You must like

football as much as I do . . . How many of you play? I know the school doesn't have a team, but you have teams of your own, don't you? The boys in Mifflin do. I read in the *Two-Village Times* just the other day that their team of juniors is trying to get up a game. I suppose you boys are going to give them one, aren't you? With the interest you're showing in football here this afternoon, I'm sure—"

Some boys near Bo said out loud, "We don't have a team. Not yet, anyway."

"Oh, you're missing all the fun!" Scotty told them. "Team play is great stuff. You'll love it! Better plan to have yourselves a team."

"There's only ten of us," a boy from Barry's neighborhood spoke out.

"We've got eleven now!" Barry jumped up shouting. He looked around at his friends as he tapped Bo on the top of the head. *"Him.* He moved across the street from me yesterday."

"There you are," Scotty said with a wave of his hand. "Eleven men and you're ready to ramble."

"We'll ramble all over Mifflin!" someone shouted. Other voices were heard. "We sure will!" "We'll show 'em who's the top team in the two villages!"

Round about him Bo could feel the excitement rising.

It was rising inside him too. "Scotty kept his promise! Scotty kept his promise!" the words sang in his head as, right before his eyes, boys were grouping themselves into teams. Most thrilling of all, *he* had become a team man. He felt as big as eleven boys rolled into one, and thought, *Who's afraid of Rodney and his Mifflins? We'll show 'em which potato is the best in the barrel!*

Then came a few bad minutes when it was discovered that so many boys wanted to meet Mifflin's challenge that the honor might fall to some other group. However, after Scotty asked questions about the boys' ages and weights, everyone agreed that in all fairness the game should be played by teams from the same grades in school.

"That's *us!*" Katie squealed. As Bo and his brand new teammates echoed her, he was positive Scotty gave him a wink. Bo almost pinched himself to make sure he wasn't dreaming. Like magic, his troubles had vanished. He was on a team and the team had determined to play Mifflin. He had nothing in the world to worry about, except to win that game. He looked up at the young man who had brought about this miracle and said to himself, "For that guy, I'd do *anything*. I would—I would—" As he tried to think of a deed noble enough to show how he felt about his hero, Mr. Ryan leaped onto the platform.

"If you'll give me the floor for a minute, Scotty," the

druggist said, "I'd like to say a word or two at this point." Scotty stepped down. Mr. Ryan began, "I just want to remind you kids that Cedarville has high standards for its athletes. Scott Freeman set those standards. From one end of our country to the other, wherever football is played, people know about Scott Freeman. They know him as a clean-living, clean-thinking young man. As a fine sportsman. As a competitor who plays the game with every ounce of his strength, yet can take both defeat and victory with a quiet smile. Scott is everybody's idea of a true hero—"

"Now wait a minute, Tom!" the hero objected from the sidelines with an embarrassed look on his face. "You're forgetting all the other football players in the United States."

"Let *their* home towns remember *them*," Mr. Ryan said, looking down at his listeners. "We will remember Scotty. Won't we, kids?"

While the shouts of "Yes! Yes!" died away, he held up the bronze football and continued, "This trophy stands in a place of honor in our public library, to remind us of the fine athletes of our community, from Scott Freeman on down through the list of other boys whose names will be engraved here in the years to come . . . Maybe yours will be one of those names . . . or yours . . . or yours." Mr. Ryan's glance rested on Bo for a moment, then passed on to another boy at the end of the row. In the hush that fell as the speaker stopped, that other boy asked out loud, "What would we have to do to get our names on that trophy?"

"You know the answer better than I do." Mr. Ryan smiled at Scotty. "Your name has been put on many a trophy. You tell him how to become a hero."

CHAPTER FOUR

Katie,
the Team Trainer

Scotty stood before them again, his red hair gleaming in the spotlight of sunbeams that poured through a hole in the roof of the rickety shelter house. He smiled and shook his head. "I'm not really a hero. And although I'm awfully proud of having my name on that trophy, I can't for the life of me tell you how it happened. All I can say to you is—do your best."

He looked from one to another as if he were speaking directly to each boy and said in a serious tone, "Never fail yourself. Always live up to the best that is in you . . . Walk your straightest. Fight your hardest. And win—or lose—by the rules."

Bo wondered at these words. They didn't sound much like team talk. Still, as he thought them over, he began to understand, especially when Scotty finished, "If each of

49

you lives up to his best in this way, you'll have a whole team of heroes . . . That is football at its finest."

Bo felt a tingle run down his spine as Scotty asked them, "Will you promise me always to play for that?"

"Yes! Yes!" "We will!" "I promise!" came the answering shouts. Bo heard Katie chant, "Cross my heart and hope to die."

He solemnly repeated to himself, "Corss my heart and dope to hie." In his excitement he did not notice what he had said.

Scotty brought them all down to earth then by saying now that they had teams, they could be expected to play games. And to be worthy of calling themselves football players, they would have to work hard to learn the game.

"Suppose we start with passing," he said. "To be a good passer, step into your throw like a baseball pitcher does. Also, it's a good idea to practice throwing while you're down on one knee. That teaches you balance, and follow-through and direction. Always throw at a target, even in practice. This will help you to develop accuracy."

He nodded at one of the high school players waiting at the far end of the platform. "Let 'er come, Billy." The boy he spoke to threw a pass. Scotty caught it, turned to the audience and said, "I am going to have Billy throw again and I want you kids to watch how he keeps the ball up. Even to get a grip on it, he never holds it below his shoulder. Like this." The ball whizzed across the platform into Billy's hands. Back it came. Scott caught it, held it close to his body and started to run but stopped short, saying, "There isn't enough room up here to demonstrate how to run with a pass. But remember to run at full speed. And always expect to be tackled. Therefore, wrap yourself around the ball so it can't be knocked out of your hands . . . Billy, you and one of your teammates stand out here and pass back and forth while I tell the others what to watch for."

As the high school players demonstrated passing, Scotty went on, "When you are on the receiving end of a pass, watch the ball all the time it is coming toward you. Keep your eyes on it until it is in your hands. Then 'put it away,' as we say. That means wrapping your arm around it and hunching your shoulder over it as you keep your hand clamped over one end. When you are running to catch a long pass, keep your hands down until you raise them to pull in the ball. This helps your running speed, because you can use your hands to pump until the very last second."

Bo found himself wondering if Rodney Sanders knew all these things about passing. "He probably does," Bo decided, "since he is Mifflin's star passer. Golly day! I hope

Barry remembers all this. There's so much to learn I'm afraid I'll forget some of it."

There was still more to learn, for Scotty talked about blocking and tackling and punting until he suddenly stopped and asked Tom Ryan, "Am I running over time?"

"Well, I did promise the mothers that all these kids would be home by four-thirty," Tom answered with a glance at his watch. "It's twenty after, now."

"That ends our work-out for today, kids," Scotty told his audience. "Go straight home. Don't dawdle on the way, so your mothers won't blame me if you are late." He smiled and waved and wished the boys good luck as football players.

They didn't want to leave. They swarmed to the platform, asking questions, begging for his autograph. In the crowd, as different boys jostled against Bo and Barry, Barry would say, "Hi, Nick," or "Jack" or "Johnny . . . This is Bo Bowling, our new man." Bo met most of the boys in this way. Presently they were standing in the push around the speaker. Scotty made Bo the most important boy there by asking him at once, "How did it go? Is everything satisfactory with you now?"

"Everything is pie and ice cream," Bo answered. He tried to keep calm but joy and excitement bubbled up in him, causing him to say as he pointed to his teammates, "Bees are the goys I'm woing to play gith."

Only Scotty seemed to notice the mistake. He gave Bo a pat on the shoulder. "So you're on a team already. Quick work, old man."

Other boys were pushing from behind to get near Scotty, so all Bo could say was "Thanks! Golly, *thanks!*" as he was swept to the edge of the crowd. There he stood while more and more members of his new team gathered about. They began calling him "Bo" as if they had known him for years. He thought them a fine bunch of fellows, and tried to learn all their names at once, which was impossible. The one named Bob Harper, who had big square shoulders, presently said something about letting the Mifflin team know Cedarville wanted to play them. "How will we get word to them," asked Jack Pancake, the tall, tangle-footed one.

"Bo knows somebody on the Mifflin team," Barry said. "Don't you, Bo? Why don't you just tell *him.*"

"Sure," Bo said, being too excited to trust himself to say anything more. His last difficulty was gone! The boys even decided to play the game on whatever Saturday in October should be agreeable to Mifflin. Less than an hour later he was settling the matter with Rodney Sanders.

"We'll play on our field," Rodney said. "Cedarville

doesn't have a decent place for kids to play football of course."

That "of course" made Bo grind his teeth. He could make no come back because Rodney was right. Cedarville's old recreation park once had a gridiron, but now it was covered with weeds and the goal posts long since had fallen.

"We'll show you a real field," Rodney repeated. "We'll show you how to play, too."

Bo said to himself, "And I'll show *you* how to tackle," thinking how much he would enjoy stopping Rodney in the middle of a long run. Later, however, he began to realize he had a lot more to learn about tackling before he would be ready to play in a game. He and Barry were talking about this on the way from school the next afternoon. At the end of his first day in Cedarville Elementary, Bo felt quite at home there. Being in the same class with Barry and some of his new teammates helped a lot. He made up his mind to be a good player so these boys wouldn't be sorry they took him in. "Let's practice punting," he suggested now as he stopped with Barry and Katie at the Hunts' front door.

Barry got the ball and the boys went to work. Katie sat on the curb and watched or chased the ball. After a while she asked if she could have a turn kicking, but they said they were in training to beat Mifflin and had to keep at it. A moment later Bo was running to catch a long punt when he skidded in the loose stones of Hunts' drive. Down he went, ripping his jeans. He came up with one knee full of pebbles and dirt and oozing blood. When he tried to walk, his leg hurt if he put any weight on it. Barry said, "Lean on me. I'll help you home so your mother can bandage that."

"Mrs. Bowling isn't home," Katie reminded them. "Mom took her to the sewing at church, remember?"

Neither mother was at home! "Wel-l-l," Bo said, drawing a long, painful breath, "I guess I'll have to take care of this myself." He looked down at his knee. It was becoming stiff. He knew nothing about dressing wounds except that they should be taken care of immediately to prevent something dangerous called infection. The thought came into his mind: *Suppose my knee is ruined for playing football.*

Katie came running with a first aid kit. She sent Barry for a basin of warm water and the green soap. "I passed my first aid tests at camp two summers before last," she said to Bo, who was impressed with the skillful way she sponged his knee. "Now the camp nurse lets me help her . . . This is going to hurt," she added as she spread some antiseptic on his cuts.

"Yow!" His leg jerked even though he tried to hold it steady. He wouldn't admit it hurt, though. All he said was, "It stings a little."

While Katie taped on a bandage he almost spoiled the job by suddenly jumping up with a shout. "I've got an idea! Why don't you be our trainer, Katie? Every team has a doctor or a trainer to take care of the players who get hurt in games. Golly day! Look what you did for me just now! I think we always ought to have you handy, even when we're only practicing. Don't you think so, Barry?"

"You're right." Barry turned to his sister, "What do *you* say?"

Although Katie looked very pleased, she let the boys coax her for several minutes before she would agree to their offer.

"You could be our water boy too," Barry said, as an added attraction.

She pretended to be insulted at this until Bo said, "Sure you could, Katie. We need somebody who knows enough not to let the players drink much during a game. They'd pay more attention to you than to one of the other boys."

"She'd make 'em mind her, all right." Barry grinned. "I can just see her carrying the bucket out to us during a time out. She'd hold it under our noses, then snatch it

56

away, and say, 'That's all you get till you make a touch-down.' "

"Who wants to drink water out of a sloppy old bucket," Katie demanded. "I ought to have one of those little carts you see at games on television."

"That's like a girl," Barry said. "Always wanting things fancy. As if a trick water cart would make us a better team."

"It wouldn't of course," Bo agreed. "But it might help us to *look* like a better team. That ought to impress the Mifflins."

"The way to impress them is to make more touchdowns than they do," Barry said. But when Katie seemed disappointed, he went to the garage and returned pulling a child's wagon. "Here's our old one, Sis. The paint's gone and one wheel wobbles, but maybe we can use it."

All they needed now was some kind of water container to set in the wagon. "Something with a cover," Katie said, "to keep out dirt and germs." She was sure they could find what they needed in the second-hand store where she sometimes went with her mother to hunt for antiques.

"Let's go look right away," suggested Bo, the man of action.

Neither of the boys had any money, so Katie brought her small red purse and they started out, pulling the wagon so they could haul home whatever they might buy. The clatter of the wobbly wheels brought Tyler running. "What you *doo-oo*-ing?" When he wanted to go with them, Katie sent him back home to ask his mother for permission. "She'll keep him there," Katie assured Bo and Barry. "She always wants him to stay in this block and not go too far from home."

Bo looked back to make sure Tyler reached home safely. He was already rather used to having the little fellow tag at his heels, needing to be watched over.

Down the street went the three with the rattling wagon. Presently Bo noticed they were passing his familiar landmark, Tom Ryan's Pharmacy. Next Katie said, "This is the library." Bo wanted to stop in for another look at the bronze football, but did not mention it because the other two had their minds on finding the second-hand store. Coming to a corner, Barry pointed down the side street to a clutter of battered chairs, old sewing machines and wash tubs on the sidewalk. "There it is."

Bo, however, had eyes only for a wooden Indian which stood at a doorway nearer by. "This is what we need," he whooped as he leaped forward and tackled the Indian around the ankles. The figure rocked on its metal platform, making such a clatter that the door opened, a long bony arm reached out, and a grimy hand grabbed the

58

Indian by its naked shoulder to steady it. A long nose followed, then a face almost as fierce as the Indian's.

"What are you doing to Nantaquas?" the man roared. For a small man he made a terrifying noise.

Bo gulped. He said in an excited squeak, "I was using it—him—for a dackling tummy."

The man's face changed. It had been angry, now it looked surprised. Bo started to explain, "What I mean is—" The man hadn't even noticed Bo's mistake. He was saying, "A tackling dummy. Hmmm. That's interesting. Where did you get the idea, boy?"

Where do ideas come from? Bo couldn't answer. Katie tried to tell the man. "Bo just took a look at that Indian and tackled it."

"So I see," the man grunted as he pushed the heavy platform back into place beside the door. He wiped his hands on his trousers before carefully running his fingers over the statue's carved brown muscles and necklace of wooden bear claws. "No damage done, I guess. Fortunately. He is quite valuable. I prize him highly."

"I didn't mean to hurt it." Bo was honestly sorry.

"Not it—him." The man frowned. "I told you his name is Nantaquas. Brother to Pocahontas. The pair of them stood outside a tobacco store over in the city when I was a little boy. Great friends of mine. Used to be plenty of wooden Indians around the country in those days."

"I never saw one before except this one," said Katie, who seemed less in awe of this man than the boys were. "There aren't any others in town, are there?"

The man shook his head. "Like real Indians, this kind have just about disappeared too. The ones left are mostly in museums. Except Nantaquas. It would be a shame to shut him in with a lot of mummies and stuffed birds. So I bought him, when I had the chance. Put him outside my shop where he can watch people come and go, like he used to do. He's chained there at the bottom—see?—so no-body can walk off with him like this." He linked arms with the wooden creature and did a jig step. They made an interesting couple—the small, gray, grease-stained man and the wooden warrior holding a bunch of painted cigars in his outstretched wooden hand.

"I didn't stop to think he might be valuable," Bo said in apology, "or I wouldn't have tackled him. I'm sorry."

"You should be sorry, for making a tackle like that." The man looked sharply at him. "You were aiming for his ankles. Dangerous place to grab a man. Nantaquas could have knocked your head clean off your neck, if he could move his legs. You should have tackled him above his knees. That's safer. Throw your shoulder into him just below his hip."

"Like this?" Forgetting himself, Bo made another dive at the wooden Indian.

"Not again!" The man whirled in front of Nantaquas, bending low and sprawling Bo on the sidewalk. Bo came up laughing. "Woop! I'm sorry. I don't know what made me do that."

"Why don't you boys tackle each other?" The man frowned at them as he drew himself erect and prepared to defend Nantaquas again if necessary.

Katie already was taking seriously her duties as team trainer. She answered, "If they tackle themselves, they'll be black and blue before they even get into a real game."

"That's the truth," Barry said.

"That's why we need a tackling dummy," Bo added. "And when I saw Nant—uh—Nanty—well, *him*—I thought—"

"You have another think a-coming," the man said. "Why don't you look in the second-hand store? You might find something there."

"We thought this was it," said Bo. "We came here to find something to put on this wagon to carry water to our football team."

Katie stepped forward to explain. "My brother and I

know the second-hand store is next door. But Bo saw the Indian first, and he—"

"What kind of store is yours, Mister?" Bo quickly changed the subject.

The man stepped aside so they could read the lettering on the dingy window beside the open door.

T. Edison MacGillicuddy

INVENTIONS

"What do you invent?" Barry asked. All three pressed their noses against the window to see inside an inventor's shop.

"Machines, mostly. Or parts of machines. Other things too. I've been inventing since I was in the cradle. That's why my father named me Thomas Edison," he said. "Though folks hardly ever call me anything but Mac."

Katie gave him a dazzling smile. "Maybe you could invent a water cart for us."

"Or some kind of tackling dummy," Barry added. "Could you do that, Mr. Mac?"

"Of course I could." Mac nodded as if to say he could invent anything he put his mind to. "But I won't. You're old enough to do some of your own inventing. You thought of using Nantaquas to practice tackling on, didn't you?"

"That was him." Katie pointed to Bo, and Mr. Mac turned to him as he finished, "You had the start of an idea there. Now think about it until you hit on something you really *can* use for your dummy."

"What about our water cart?" Katie persisted.

Mr. MacGillicuddy squinted at the junk piled in front of the shop next door. He scratched his ear and said, "Only this morning I saw an article there which would suit your purpose to a T."

"What is it? What is it?" all three shouted at once.

He shook his head. "I shan't tell you. I'm plumb against helping folks, young or old, who don't try to help themselves. But—" he held up one finger when they looked disappointed, "—mind you, if you use your brains and find the right thing, I'll fasten it onto your wagon for you."

"You will! Oh, Mr. Mac, you're the nicest man we know!" Katie beamed at him. Barry said, "We never once thought about having to fasten it, did we, Bo?"

Bo answered that in his opinion inventors were smarter than any other kind of people.

"Let's see how smart *you* are," said T. Edison MacGillicuddy. "Go next door and make your purchase. And don't give over a dollar for it."

CHAPTER FIVE

The Tackling Dummy

At the second-hand store, the first article which seemed suitable for water carrying was a huge crock. Barry was ready to buy it. So was Katie, even though she said it should have some kind of cover. Bo held back. "An old crock on a wobbly wagon isn't good enough for our team," he said. "Let's look for something better."

He found the very thing under a table stacked with dishes. It was a small-sized metal urn of the kind used for coffee-making at drugstore lunch counters. Katie was delighted with the little faucet at the bottom. "I can fill paper cups and hand them out to you boys. That will be *very* sanitary. After we scrub this, of course," she said, poking her head into the urn.

Barry, who also looked into it, announced there was a hole in the bottom. For this reason the youngsters refused

65

to pay the storekeeper the two dollars he asked. "Besides, Mr. Mac told us not to pay over a dollar," they said.

The storekeeper sighed and shrugged his shoulders. "It's yours for a buck then. What Mac says around here, goes."

While Katie took the money from her red pocketbook, Bo and her brother promised to pay their share later and went to the inventor's shop carrying the urn between them.

"Is this it, Mr. Mac?" they called out.

The inventor pretended to be annoyed that he had made a bad bargain and now must drop his other work to keep his promise to them. But Bo noticed how eagerly he took measurements of both urn and wagon, and rummaged in dusty corners of his shop, whistling and murmuring about braces and angle irons. Not finding what he was looking for, he said, "Leave your wagon and I'll have it ready for you later."

Katie said rather timidly, "The urn has a hole in it. Can you fix that too?"

Bo told her, "Of course he can. Inventors can fix anything. Can't they, Mr. Mac?"

The answer came from inside the urn where Mr. Mac had stuck his head to investigate. "I certainly wouldn't let this hole stop me. On the other hand, I'll stop *it*."

While he was still chuckling at his own joke, Bo dared mention a tackling dummy again. "We really do need one, Mr. Mac," he said.

"Stay away from Nantaquas," Mac muttered.

"Oh, sure," Bo said quickly.

Mac threw him a keen glance. "Thought I told you I'd help only on one condition. You have to show me first that you're willing to help yourselves . . . Now think, what does a tackling dummy look like and what kind of stuff is it made of?"

"I never saw one," said Katie. Bo and Barry hadn't either, except in pictures. Bo tried to think what it reminded him of. "A laundry bag!" he said. "That's it! A laundry bag stuffed so full that it's very hard. Say, Mr. Mac, why couldn't we make a bag like that—a long skinny one?"

The inventor looked pleased but said nothing, allowing Bo to continue, "We could hang it from—from a tree, I suppose. I don't think we could build a regular framework to swing it from . . . No, I think a good stout limb of a tree would do all right."

"Now you're thinking like T. Edison himself," Mac complimented Bo. "A strong canvas bag, well stuffed, is a fine idea. Perhaps your mother could run one up for you on her sewing machine."

"If your mother can't, ours can," Katie put in.

"And we could hang it from the big tree in our front yard. That would be a swell place!" Bo thought how much fun it would be to have a bunch of boys playing under his own tree.

"Think of your parents," Mr. Mac suggested. "They might not like having the lawn torn up." He advised the boys to use the big tree at the old recreation park.

Bo remembered that tree. "It's even bigger than the one in my yard," he said.

A gleam came into Mac's eyes. "There are only a few of those noble ones left any more. They're all that remains of the great forest that once covered this land. It's a good thing we have 'em too—to remind us to grow straight and strong and to stand unafraid in the storms."

"And to hang tackling dummies from," Barry added.

"Oh, I suppose so." Although the inventor spoke rather grumpily, Bo hoped he meant he would help them put up their dummy.

First, though, they had to produce the thing. Bo's mother, when he asked her, said she had a piece of canvas just the right size. In no time at all she sewed it into a huge sausage ready to be stuffed. Then Mrs. Hunt had to be called to the rescue to bring old rags to help fill it. What a lot of worn-out shirts and dresses and sheets and pillow slips and towels Barry and Katie and Bo packed into that canvas bag! "Remember, it has to be hard and solid as a real live football player," Mr. Mac had told them.

When it was finished, true to his promise, he gathered ropes and pulleys from his shop and went with the boys to the big tree in the old park where he helped them hang the dummy from one of the stout lower branches. Katie, who tagged after them, asked if they could safely leave the dummy there.

"Who would disturb it?" Mac asked. "Hardly anybody comes here any more."

"They used to play football here, didn't they?" Bo pointed to the wide, flat space not far from the river bank. "Why did they give up and let the field go to weeds?"

"This bottom land gets too muddy for football during the fall rains," Mr. Mac explained. "It could be drained easy enough, though. You'd think the Cedarville Boosters and the PTA's and some of the other clubs would get together and fix it up for the kids. 'Twouldn't cost much. All they need, probably, is for somebody to start the ball rolling."

With the dummy now ready for use, Bo and Barry and their teammates began spending their after-school time at the old recreation field. They lined up and took turns making a dash, grabbing the dummy and pretending it was a Mifflin player. "Knock the stuffing out of him!" they encouraged one another. To Bo's secret satisfaction, the dummy held together although Katie predicted it would not last much longer. She usually followed the boys to practice, trundling her water cart behind her.

Mr. Mac had said she might keep it at his shop, which was handy to the field. So each afternoon she arrived with her darling, its little tank shining bright and gurgling with fresh water for the team. She even had paper cups, kept in one of the small compartments which the inventor had built at the end of the wagon, to her great delight. Later, she planned, she also would keep first aid supplies

there. With Mr. Mac's help she had already painted the wagon and straightened its wobbly wheels so that, in her eyes at least, it had taken on the appearance of a field ambulance.

After a whole week of tackling the dummy between sessions of punting and passing, the boys felt they were well on the way to victory over Mifflin. Bo was quite set back when Rodney Sanders telephoned to ask for Cedarville's line-up for the game.

"Line-up?" Bo repeated, wondering how he and his men could have been so stupid as to forget this important thing.

"Sure. Line-up." Rodney spelled it out, adding, "If you know what the word means."

Bo ignored this sarcasm. He asked, "Why do you want to know our line-up now? The game isn't until—"

"I need it for the *Two-Village Times*," Rodney cut in. "The editor wants to know who plays each position on your team. What do you want me to tell him? That you dopes don't know the difference between center and end?"

Bo thought quickly. "I'll call you back about this later. Tomorrow," he added, putting down the phone before Rodney could ask more questions.

Now that a line-up had been mentioned, Bo realized the reason Cedarville didn't have one was because they had not yet practiced any team plays. "We'll have to start that at once," he decided. But first came the business of a line-up. He talked to the others about it at recess next day, finding out what positions they thought they could play best. He himself intended to be an end—right or left didn't matter to him—until he learned the Nelson brothers wanted very much to play those two positions. Next he thought he might do well at guard or tackle. But Barry and several more pointed out that he knew more about the game than most of them and therefore should be in a position where he could handle the ball more. By that time he thought he'd wait and take whatever spot was left open.

The center, everybody agreed, should be Dick Maull, who was big yet quick and dependable. Barry was everyone's choice for quarterback although he kept insisting he wasn't smart enough. "But you can run faster than any of us. And you can pass," they said. "You're our best prospect for quarterback."

"Well, I'll play there if Bo thinks I can," Barry said.

Bo nodded. Someone else also wanted his opinion. Bob Harper asked, "Who would be better at fullback—Jack Pancake or me?"

"You, Bob," Bo decided instantly. Harper was all muscle. When you tackled him you thought you'd run into a road roller. Bo knew! Jack couldn't compare with Harper as a back. To tell the truth, tall, thin, rattle-brained Jack wasn't much of a player. But men were scarce and the two halfback positions were still vacant, so Bo assigned Jack to one and himself to the other. "Now let's see how our line-up looks on paper," he said, pulling an old spelling list from his pocket and writing on the back of it:

LINE

Ends	John and Nick Nelson
Tackles	Zuber and Henderson
Guards	Krutsky and Norwood
Center	Maul

Quarterback	Hunt
Fullback	Harper
Halfbacks	Pancake and Bowling

"There are two l's in my name," Dick Maull said, reading over Bo's shoulder. The correction was made.

Everybody agreed on the line-up. "Great! . . . Looks good to me!" They slapped one another on the back, cheering, "Bring on your Mifflin! We've got a team!"

Next they had to learn some plays. But how? Even Bo, who seemed to know so much about football, was sure of only one thing about plays. "There are two kinds," he said. "Offensive plays, to use when you have the ball and want to score. And defensive plays, to keep the other team from making touchdowns."

"I've seen football plays printed in the newspapers," Zuber said. "Nothing but a bunch of O's and X's. I can't make heads nor tails out of 'em."

"Me either," said several others. It seemed to Bo that the team needed help. The time had come to call Scott Freeman.

That night he looked up the number in the phone book, dialed and asked for Scotty. "Speaking!" said a voice Bo remembered with a thrill.

"This is Bo Bowling—the boy you talked to at the shelter house Sunday. Early in the afternoon, before the football meeting began and the bleachers weren't set up yet. Do you remember?"

"Sure I remember," Scott replied. "How are you getting along with that team we started?"

"Fine," Bo said, "except that we've struck a snag. We're going to play Mifflin about three weeks from now and we don't know any teamwork."

"Not any?"

"We've practiced passing and receiving. And blocking and tackling of course. But we need some plays for making touchdowns."

"I can see that," Scott agreed.

"I got a book at Ryan's drugstore," Bo said. "Five Hundred Winning Football Plays. It wasn't any help."

"Those are meant for coaches. What you kids want is one simple play that's easy to learn and hard for the other team to stop."

"That's exactly it! Could—could you teach us one like that?" Bo knew he was asking a lot, but his team's need was desperate and he didn't know anyone else to turn to. His father and Barry's both had offered to help, but he could imagine how Rodney would laugh to hear Cedarville was coached by a father. "Mifflin is coached by a real football player, the boys say," he explained to Scotty. "Do you suppose you *could* show us a good play?"

"I'd be glad to if I were going to be here. You see, I just happen to be home overnight. I have to be back at the University in time for football practice tomorrow. Classes are starting too, so I won't get home to Cedarville again until Thanksgiving," Scott said. "Still, I could draw a diagram of a play and write some instructions for you. Do you think you could follow them?"

"We sure would try!" Bo said. "That would be a big help and we'd appreciate it lots."

"Okay. I'll fix you up."

Bo thanked him and was about to put down the phone when Scott said, "Hold on a minute. How am I going to get this to you?"

Bo offered to come for it at once if Scotty would tell him how to get there. Scott said he wouldn't have the play worked out until past Bo's bedtime, but he had an idea. "Did you ever hear of Mr. MacGillicuddy, the inventor?"

"Do you know Mr. Mac too?" Bo asked.

"Do I know him?" A chuckle came over the wire. "You ask him about the time he caught me tackling his wooden Indian, when I was your age."

"He caught me at it too." Bo joined in the laugh.

Then Scotty said, "I'll leave your football play with

Mac on my way back to college tomorrow morning. Good-bye now, and good luck to you," he ended. "Take care of football here in Cedarville while I'm gone."

"We will! We'll knock the socks off Mifflin! We'll make you proud of us," Bo promised.

"It's *how* you win that matters most," Scotty replied. "Nearly any game can be won by cheating or dirty play. But fight hard and play by the rules, and I'll be proud of you even if you lose. Better still, you'll be proud of yourselves."

Bo remembered Scotty had said almost these same words to him once before. He was ashamed he had forgotten them. They made him see this football game was more than simply a chance to set back the boastful Mifflin team. It was a glorious time for the younger boys in Cedarville to show they were worthy to wear the football shoes a great player had left behind. "You can count on us," Bo promised both himself and Scotty before putting down the phone.

CHAPTER SIX

Mr. Mac's Mystery Coach

Next morning on his way to school Bo raced to the inventor's shop. He flung open the door panting, "Mr. Mac! Mr. Mac! Did Frotty Sceeman weave something lith you for me?"

"Wup, wup," Mac said in soothing tones. "Back up and come again, easy like."

Bo took a deep breath, swallowed and repeated in straighter words. Mac said he hadn't opened the shop more than two minutes ago and Bo was the first person to drop in. "Bust in, I should say," he corrected himself.

Bo was too distressed to notice Mac's small grin. "Scotty said he would leave me a diagram of a football play," he explained. "He had to start early this morning to go back to college, and on his way out of town he said he was going to stop here and leave it."

78

Mac nodded in a calm way. "He probably left it with Nantaquas."

"Nantaquas?" Bo wasn't sure he had understood. He pointed out the door at the Indian. "Him?"

"Sure. All my friends leave messages with him when the shop's locked," Mac said. "They just roll up the paper and stick it in the hole in his head. Many wooden Indians have holes in their heads, you know."

"They do?" Bo began to wonder if he had a hole in his own head because none of this conversation made sense to him.

"Some people say that's how the wood is protected from weathering. Oil is supposed to be poured into the hole every now and then," Mac said. "Let's go take a look and see if Nantaquas has got anything in his hair besides wooden feathers."

Bo ran outdoors. A slim tube of paper stood atop the Indian's head. Bo balanced on the doorstep to reach over and draw out the tiny roll of paper. "He did leave the diagram," he told Mac as he spread out the slightly oil-stained sheets. "Look! And he wrote directions how to make touchdowns with it too. Number 33, it's called. Wait till I show the fellows." He dashed out of the shop with a "Thanks, Mr. Mac. Much obliged, Nantaquas!" and ran all the way to school.

At recess the team gathered round to study the diagram of O's and X's arranged like this:

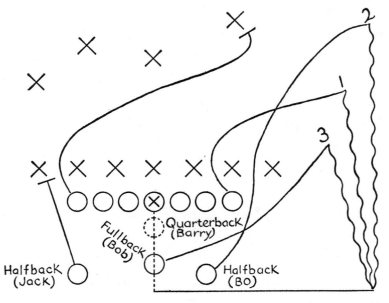

NOTE: *In a game, the quarterback and pass-receivers usually won't have time to run this far to the side. Nor will the receivers be able to go so deep into enemy territory. I spread them out here to make the diagram more clear to you. Scotty*

Bo read aloud what Scott Freeman had written: *"On this play the quarterback*—that's you, Barry—*takes the ball from center and steps back. The left halfback*—that's Jack—*blocks the enemy end who is coming across to try to stop our quarterback. Our end cuts through the enemy*

80

line and goes way down into their territory. Our right halfback—that's me—does the same, only he goes farther still. Our fullback—Bob Harper—also crosses over and waits, or else runs with the ball if quarterback has given it to him." Bo stopped reading to follow these instructions on the chart. "Hey, look what that does! It gives Barry three fellows to pass to. Bob Harper, Nick Nelson or me."

Barry studied the diagram more closely. "Mmmm. I see. But how will I know which one to throw to?"

Bo read on: *"Chances are, one or two of these men will have enemy blockers after them. Quarterback should throw to the man who is open to receive.*

Barry was still looking at the diagram. "You know what, Bo? We sure could fool Mifflin with this play. They'd see us have three players getting ready to catch my pass, and they'd figure they could stop us by intercepting the ball. So they'd all run over to that side. Then I'd fool 'em by keeping the ball myself and running with it. How about that?"

"Great!" Bo looked up from the paper he was reading. "That's exactly what Scotty says here you should do."

"I'd run along the side of the field there—" Barry pointed to a dotted line on the diagram, "—and you fellows who were going to catch my pass—"

"We'll block for you instead," put in Nick Nelson, the end.

Bo could fairly see Barry skipping toward the Mifflin goal line with the ball while he himself stopped Rodney Sanders with a powerful block. It was Katie who brought the boys back to business by offering to make copies of the diagram so everybody could have one to learn as quickly as possible. After a few days of practicing the play, the team began to see it needed more help than Scott Freeman's Number 33.

"I do wish Scotty would be our coach," Bo said to Barry and Katie as they left the old football field together. "But I guess he has all he can handle, playing big-time college football and studying his lessons too."

"Let's beg him real hard," was Katie's plan. "Then maybe he'll find time to help us."

Bo and Barry did not think so, but they agreed to ask Mr. Mac what he thought. So, with Katie pulling her water cart, they went to the shop.

"Hi, Nantaquas!" Bo slapped the Indian's arm as they opened the door.

Mac, who was testing a transistor, looked up to say, "Well, well, if it isn't Florence Nightingale and the Galloping Ghosts."

Bo glanced around to make sure who was behind him.

82

It was only Katie, who said, "I know who Florence Nightingale was. She went to war and nursed the soldiers a long time ago."

Mac looked wise. "Football players need somebody to bind up their wounds too. And to bring them a drink of cool water."

"That's our Katie! But who were the Galloping Ghosts?" the boys asked.

"There was only one, really. He was Red Grange, who played football for Illinois years ago. He got the nickname of Galloping Ghost because he had a spooky way of running through the opposing team's line without anybody being able to stop him."

Bo wanted to hear more about Red Grange, but Katie jumped in and said the team needed a coach and did Mr. Mac think Scotty Freeman would have time to do it.

"I doubt it." Mac shook his head. "Besides, he's seventy-five miles from here most of the season. Why don't you try somebody closer home? How about one of the men teachers at your school?"

"There's only Mr. Wheery, who teaches science," Barry answered. "Some of the boys already asked him. They found out he hardly knows a first down from an end run."

"How about Tom Ryan? He played football once," said Mac.

"He did say he might help us," Barry admitted. "But we want somebody who seems more like a real coach."

"Mr. Ryan always has on that white coat," Katie explained. This made no sense to Bo, who wondered how she could be so smart sometimes and so dumb at other times.

"How about Nantaquas?" Mac suggested with a solemn nod toward the door. "The one play your team has, came out of his head."

Katie giggled. The boys thought she didn't help matters when she said, "You're an inventor, Mr. Mac. Why don't you invent a coach for us?"

Mac looked at her, then at Bo and Barry, while he seemed to consider this suggestion. He nodded slowly. "That's an idea. An . . . interesting . . . idea. By gumbo, I might just have a try at it!"

Bo repeated this conversation at the dinner table that evening. He laughed. "I wonder what kind of a coach Mr. Mac will invent for us. Something like Nantaquas, I suppose. Nantaquas is a wooden Indian," he explained to his parents. "He's in front of Mr. MacGillicuddy's."

"Who is this Mr. Mac?" Dad asked. "How did you kids get so thick with him?"

"We met him when we were making Katie's water

wagon. I told you about it. And he helped with our tackling dummy. Now—" Bo laughed again at the thought, "—he says he is going to try and invent us a coach."

"Why don't you let Daddy coach you, as he offered to do," Mother said. "He played football in college. So did Barry's father. Mrs. Hunt told me he too had offered to help you boys. Surely you'd rather have dads coaching—"

"No, they wouldn't," Dad snapped. "They'd rather have a wooden Indian. Obviously."

"His name isn't Obviously. It's Nantaquas," Bo said.

He looked so serious his father smiled and said, "Okay, son. You choose your own coach. However, I do think Mr. Hunt and I should meet this inventor fellow. I'd like to make sure you kids aren't being a nuisance to him. No doubt Barry's father feels the same way."

Of course Bo and Barry didn't really think Mr. Mac could invent a coach for them, yet on their way to and from football practice they stopped at his shop to pry him with questions. "What is our coach going to look like?" "When will he be ready?" "How soon can we meet him?"

"You will never meet him face to face," Mac told them one day.

Barry laughed. "Who is he—another Galloping Ghost?"

Bo saw the inventor was serious. He asked, "What is his name?"

"Teneyes," Mac said. "Coach Teneyes."

"Coach Ten-eyes," Bo repeated. He thought this was another of Cedarville's odd names. After Shingledecker and Weatherwax and Pancake, which was the name of one of his teammates, Teneyes seemed to fit right in.

"Have you ever seen this Coach Teneyes?" Barry was asking.

Mac looked surprised and slightly annoyed. "That's not important. What you ought to be concerned with is: Has he seen you?"

"Well, has he?"

Mac nodded. "Sure. Why else do you think he has agreed to coach you? He says you need to be told, for one thing, to stop using your hands or arms when you block. If you keep on doing that in practice, you're sure to do it in a game. Then it can cost you a fifteen-yard penalty."

Bo stared. Until this moment he had thought Mac was only joking about an invented coach. Either that, or he meant to play the part himself. Yet, Bo now realized, the boys *had* been using their hands in blocking, and no purely imaginary coach could possibly have known it. Mac couldn't have seen them do it either, because he never had watched them practice. Even if he might possibly have

sneaked over to the old recreation park and hidden behind the big tree or one of the shelter house posts, he still couldn't have seen how they blocked. For they mostly practiced blocking only by two's and three's at home or in their schoolyard.

After all this had gone through his mind, Bo asked, "Did—did—Coach Teneyes say anything else about our blocking?"

"He said for you to keep your heads up. Make sure you're going straight into the other guy. And pull your hands in close to your chest and keep them there. Relax when you fall too, that's another thing to remember."

As Barry, too, realized they had been doing it wrong, he and Bo nodded at each other. Maybe this coach would be a big help to the team, after all. One thing more they wanted to know. "How is he going to tell us what to do, if we never see him to talk to? Will he send us directions through you?"

"If he can reach me," Mac said. "I'm out of the shop a lot. He'll probably have to communicate with you mostly through Nantaquas."

Bo remembered the message Scotty had left for him. "Oh-oh!" he said. "I'll bet Scott Freeman is our coach!"

"He told you himself he didn't have time for the job, didn't he?" Mac settled the matter.

The boys had still one more question. "Does this coach know we are playing Mifflin?"

Mac nodded and turned back to his work as if he had spent enough time on other people's problems. The boys left, in a hurry to tell their teammates.

The next day was Wednesday, the day the *Two-Village Weekly Times* was delivered. Bo grabbed it the instant it was thrown on the front step. He turned to the sports page to see if his team's line-up was there. "Here we are," he said to himself. In the lower corner, under the heading MIFFLIN vs. CEDARVILLE he read: *Among junior football players, the big game of the season will take place a week from Saturday at 10 a.m. between Cedarville and Mifflin, according to Captain Rodney Sanders of the Mifflin team. Sanders says the game will decide the championship of the two villages.*

"How do you like that!" Bo said aloud. "According to Captain Rodney Sanders! He must think he's the whole Associated Press, giving out news."

There was no more to the story except the two line-ups. Bo looked for his own name at halfback. This was the first time he had seen it in print and he was pleased with the way it looked. He checked over the names of his teammates to make sure they also were spelled correctly. Having the line-up in the paper made him feel the importance of the game. It wasn't just a bunch of kids playing in an empty schoolyard. It was "the big game of the season . . . to decide the championship of the two villages." It would decide something else too, although the paper did not say so. It would decide whether Bo and his teammates were good enough to carry on the football tradition set in Cedarville by Scott Freeman.

No wonder Bo began to feel a little scared. He had started all this with his rash words to Rodney. He felt even worse when it dawned on him that Mifflin had set the date for their game as early as possible. His team had only a few more days to prepare for it.

The Cedarville boys spent those days drilling on their one play until they could fall into position the instant they heard "Thirty-three." Still, Bo knew they would not be so sharp with Mifflin lined up in front of them. And they hadn't mastered tackling yet. And they couldn't even hold one another with their blocks. They needed more time for practice!

Some of the team muttered that they needed a coach too. Bo and most of the boys did not agree. Coach Teneyes—whoever or whatever he was—had sent them a number of bulletins correcting their mistakes and telling them how to improve. This led them to think he might appear at the game and sit on their bench to give advice.

"Do you think he will?" Bo asked Mac after their last practice on Friday.

Mac said, "No."

"Didn't he even leave any final instructions for us?" Bo asked.

"Not with me, he didn't," Mac said. "Have you checked with Nantaquas?"

When Bo stepped outside to look, there was a tiny roll of paper in the finger-size hole in the top of the Indian's wooden head. He spent the rest of the evening telephoning his teammates to read them the message typed on the paper. It was headed:

THINGS TO DO BEFORE THE GAME

1. Eat a hearty breakfast three to four hours before game time.

2. Don't think about the game. Don't worry about fumbling. Don't be scared you'll make a mistake. Forget you ever heard of football. Play checkers with your kid brother or sister. If you don't have a brother or sister, play solitaire, or another quiet game. Don't run around and use up your strength. You'll need all of it later.

3. If your legs begin to feel like rubber and your mouth is so dry you can't spit, yawn a couple of times and

take a few long, deep breaths . . . Don't worry if you feel sick. Lots of athletes feel this way before a game. It is called buck fever, but you don't have any fever at all. The sickness will go away as soon as you start to play.

"It is signed 'Coach Teneyes' with a red crayon," Bo always added as he finished reading this letter over the phone. The boys seemed to think their coach was really Mac or some of his friends. The fact that Mac wouldn't admit it struck them as being just another of those grown-up ways of doing things which don't make sense to boys. Since they couldn't get any satisfaction out of the inventor, they either had to take this kind of coaching or have none at all. For this reason the team had stopped asking questions and now were quite eager to get all the help they could from the instructions which came to them through Nantaquas.

The next morning after Bo had read the latest bulletin to his men, he had to read it again to Barry, who called groaning, "I'm too sick to play this morning, Bo. Something's the matter with me. I feel awful in my stomach."

"Did you eat a hearty breakfast as we were supposed to do?" Bo demanded.

"Oh, yes." Barry groaned louder than ever. "It's jumping around inside of me."

Katie came on the line to say, "He feels awful! I took his temperature though, and he doesn't have any fever."

"Then you're all right," Bo said to Barry with a sigh of relief. "You've just got buck fever. Remember what Coach wrote us about that? Wait, I'll read it to you again."

Bo was sorry for Barry. Yet he was pleased he himself felt fine. No buck fever for him! However, the more he thought about the game and how much he wanted to win for Scott Freeman, the more uneasy he became. An hour later he too was jumpy and upset. He wondered if Scotty ever felt this way before a game. "Fight your hardest," Scotty had said. Did he mean you had to fight hard in the game and also fight against this sick-scared feeling beforehand? *He probably did,* Bo thought. *What a lot of fight it takes to be a football player!*

CHAPTER SEVEN

Anything Can Happen
in Football

Mrs. Bowling and the Nelson boys' mother each took a carload of players to Mifflin. Katie, who had worried how to transport her water cart, went with Barry in Mr. Mac's pick-up truck. Little Tyler went with them. "I'm the only extra man our team has," he told Mac.

As Bo once had said, "Tyler is our whole scrub team. I guess we'll have to call him Scrubby and let him sit on our bench." The name stuck, just as Scrubby himself stuck to the team. He had become their mascot and Katie's assistant. Now he was on the spot to help unload her cart when Mac dropped his passengers at the Mifflin football field on his way to install a new part he had invented for a machine in a factory nearby.

"I wish I weren't too busy to stay and see our boys play," he said to Katie. "Look for me back in time to

94

pick up you and the Nightingale wagon. And while I'm gone, don't let Mifflin walk over you."

At first Bo was disappointed Mac couldn't stay with them as if he were their coach, although he didn't look much like one, being small and gray and having no more muscle than a match stick. However, Rodney Sanders's celebrated coach turned out to be merely a high school boy who wasn't even on the team. So Bo no longer felt his men were at a disadvantage in having no advisor present, especially after Mr. Mac did them an important service before leaving. He discovered Mifflin, as the home team, had not appointed a timekeeper.

"You'll need a stop watch too," Mac said, unstrapping his own watch from his wrist. "This has a timer on it, but I don't want any kid fooling with it. Therefore I appoint Mrs. Bowling head timekeeper." With a bow, he handed her his watch, showed her how to use it, and drove off. Timekeeper Bowling at once proved her ability by calling for the officials to get the game started. There was only one official—the referee, who was the same older boy who also coached Mifflin. He now called for the Cedarville captain to meet with Rodney for the toss.

The Cedarville boys had to think fast. They had been working so hard as a team, they hadn't felt the need of choosing a captain. Bo had rather hoped he would be it when they finally decided, but he knew that as a new-comer he would have to prove himself before he could expect the others to trust him to lead them. Now when someone suggested Barry, he agreed with a cheer and helped shove the hesitant little quarterback onto the field. The referee tossed a coin, Rodney won and chose to kick off, contrary to shouts from his bench. The teams lined up. Mrs. Bowling called "Time!" The ball rose into the air and Bo, watching it, ran toward it as it came down in front of him. He carried it three yards before a red-jersied Mifflin man crossed in front of him and wrapped a pair of long arms around his knees. "Ungh!" he grunted with surprise as he hit the ground. He felt as if all his bones had been jarred loose. At the same time he remembered to clamp the ball closer to his body so it couldn't be knocked out of his arms. Two or three Mifflin players fell on top of him—needlessly, he thought. They must have known the ball was dead and play stopped when Red Jersey brought him down. Finally the referee came to unscramble the tangled arms and legs and bodies. For one awful moment Bo thought he heard his mother calling, "Harold! Harold! Are you hurt?"

He scrambled to his feet as soon as he was free, kicking with one leg then the other, while waving his arms to show her he was unharmed. Fortunately this seemed to convince her. He was spared the shame of having his mother stop the game because her son was getting roughed up. In fact she must have understood his gestures very clearly, for throughout the rest of the game her performance as timekeeper was as cool-headed as if she never had seen any of the players before.

After that kick-off, with the ball in Cedarville's possession on their thirty-yard line, Bo and his teammates decided in the huddle to save Number 33 until later. Their plan was to use it to surprise the enemy after leading them to think victory would be easy. This was the time to hit the line. Jack Pancake said, "Give the ball to me. I'll carry it through." Bo, who felt Jack was the weakest spot in the backfield, made a point of being where he could rescue the ball if necessary.

The play did not get that far, however, for just as Barry reached under the center for the ball, the referee called a penalty. "Cedarville offside." Nicky Nelson had leaped across the line of scrimmage before the play started. At least, so the referee claimed. Nick and Lyle Zuber, playing next to him at tackle, both believed Nick had not moved forward until the ball was snapped, but weren't positive enough to argue. Cedarville was penalized five yards. The same thing happened twice more in the second quarter, with the result that the Cedarville boys got together at their bench between halves of the game and decided to be especially careful not to break any rule during the last half. "Then if that referee calls a penalty on us, we'll argue till we're blue in the face, and finally make him back down," Bo said.

"Yes! We'll make him back down," echoed little Scrubby, who was assisting Katie at the water cart.

As the boys talked together, they realized that in spite of what they considered unfair treatment from the referee, they were holding their own in the game. Mifflin was ahead in number of first downs made, but each time a Mifflin man had broken away toward the goal line, big Bo or one of the fleet-footed Nelson brothers had put a stop to the run. They wiped their faces on Katie's towels and trotted out to start the second half, feeling strong and full of confidence.

Bo was learning from experience to watch every move made by the other team. How exciting it was to figure out whether they intended to run to the right side of the line or to the left! And to deduce who would carry the ball! Then to meet him as he came around—*whammy!* Again and again a Mifflin player would dodge through the line and think he was headed for the goal, only to run into Bo's terrific tackle.

Bo was having the time of his life. Who thought of

buck fever now? Certainly not he. Going down with a spine-cracking jar, he came up snorting fire. "Shove in there, Krutsky! . . . Clobber him, Bob!" he encouraged his teammates, while he defied the enemy with shouts of, "What makes you think you can play football?"

Grunting, pushing, he let himself go limp as a protection against the bone-shaking jolt that came with each tackle. Yet for all his valor, his team was not able to keep the ball from the enemy. With their greater experience they were out-playing Cedarville. At this rate, Mifflin was sure to score. Only two or three times did Cedarville have the ball long enough to try Number 33. It didn't work so well as in practice. Bo handled his assignment perfectly—he always got out into the open, past the Mifflin end, whom he once blocked to protect Barry. But his teammates were not quick enough to keep other Mifflin men from stopping Barry before he could pass. Bo still had faith in 33, though. "If we block faster for Barry, I believe we can stop them," he said.

"It looks like we can't stop them any way at all," a couple of linemen muttered.

Bo told them, "Let's not give up before we're licked. *Anything* can happen in football."

The game went into the last quarter without a score on either side. The Mifflin boys, who had picked Cedarville as a pushover, grew angry because they couldn't score. Angriest of all was their captain, Rodney Sanders. The more often he was stopped by Bo, the more he refused to let anyone else carry the ball. The game settled down almost to a battle between the two boys. "I'll show you," Rodney snarled as Bo stopped him again on the twenty-five yard line. Bo didn't answer, saving his strength. He watched Mifflin come out of a long huddle. *They must be arguing with Rodney,* he thought. Then—*Rodney won.*

From the way Mifflin lined up Bo knew they were trying the same play once more. Probably this was one reason he was easily thrown off balance when he relaxed his

grip after bringing Rodney to his knees. Instantly Rodney struggled free and started running with the ball. The Mifflin crowd went crazy, yelling, "Touchdown! Touchdown!" long after Rodney had crossed the goal line with the ball.

Bo protested to the referee. "Rodney touched the ground with his knees. I'm sure of it." The official paid no attention to him, which made Bo boil with anger and excitement. "The slay was popped right there," he insisted, pointing to the spot on the field, too excited to notice what he said.

The referee threw him a puzzled glance, then shook

his head. "Rodney broke loose and kept on going, didn't he? The touchdown counts."

"It doesn't!" Bo insisted. Both teams gathered around and joined in the argument. "Wherever the ball carrier is stopped, the play stops right there. That's the way we've always seen it," the Cedarville boys agreed.

"You're wrong," said the referee. "In my rule book, it says—"

"Perhaps you are using an old rule book," Mrs. Bowling suggested. "That rule was changed quite a while ago."

"We understand how you feel, Mrs. Bowling. But the referee plays football himself. Doesn't he, fellows?" a Mifflin player spoke up.

His teammates shouted, "Sure he does! The touchdown counts!"

Bo shut his lips firmly. What could he or his teammates do? They took some childish satisfaction in cheering when Rodney missed his kick for the point-after-touchdown. Bo was immediately sorry for this show of poor sportsmanship. "It puts us in the same class with Mifflin," he said. He tried to start a rally. "Let's run old 33 once more. What have we got to lose?" The words were barely out of his mouth when the timekeeper called, "Game is over!"

Rodney came running up to clap him on the back.

"Nice game, Bo. You fellows don't play half bad. You gave us a pretty fair workout."

Bo didn't mind losing—or thought he didn't—but he resented being cheated out of his chance to win, even though the chance was slim. That wasn't football! He was so furious he didn't trust himself to speak. He shrugged and walked on toward the timekeeper. Rodney got ahead of him even there, Bo thought bitterly. He heard the other boy say, "Aunt Madge, won't you and Bo come over to our house and celebrate? Mother said to be sure and ask you."

Bo gave a silent cheer for his mother. "Thank you, Rodney," said she, "but I promised to bring these boys straight home after the game. Please tell your mother I'll come to see her some other time."

At once Mrs. Bowling filled her car with downhearted players and headed for Cedarville. Bo was glad to get away so promptly. He didn't want to talk about the game, not even to Mr. Mac. He still felt this way when his father came home from the city late in the afternoon.

"How did your game come out, Harold?" was the first thing Dad asked.

"We lost," Bo said. "They cheated."

"Now, now," said Dad. "That's not the way for a good sportsman to talk."

"But they did cheat, Dad. Ask Mom, if you don't believe me." Bo told the story. After he finished, his father agreed. "You boys behaved very well under the circumstances, I think. And so did your mother." He smiled and kissed his wife. "I'm surprised you didn't spank the whole Mifflin team, dear."

She laughed. "I felt like it. But I didn't want Harold to be ashamed of me . . . Besides, I couldn't blame those Mifflin kids too much. They really didn't understand what they were doing. They hadn't played enough to know the rules and realize how important they are."

"I agree," Dad said. "Anyway, Harold, your team got experience playing a real game. You can look around for other—"

"We sure will!" Bo muttered, eager to let the subject drop. He was somewhat soured on football at the moment. By night he was back to normal when Barry and Katie came over with their parents. Naturally there was some talk about the boys' game. Mr. Hunt explained to the young players about football rules, why they are made, and how the National Rules Committee decides upon them.

"A good example is the way the rules once were changed to make it plain that a player must carry the ball in his *hands*," Mr. Bowling put in.

Mr. Hunt nodded. "I always heard that was done because of the famous hidden-ball play with which the great Jim Thorpe and the Carlisle Indians beat Yale, back in the early days of college football," he said. "I don't know whether that is true or not."

"I can tell you a story about that—" Mr. Bowling settled back as the youngsters sprawled on the floor around his chair. "When my uncle went to Otterbein College about 1912, his coach was a man who had played on that very Carlisle team. The fellow was an Indian with a long name which the boys abbreviated to Ex. Coach Ex, they called him. He actually had played with Jim Thorpe on the team which came East and used that hidden-ball play."

The two boys, and even Katie, weren't missing a word. Mr. Hunt leaned forward to ask, "Did your uncle ever find out how they worked that play, Bowling?"

Mr. Bowling nodded. "Ex told him the Indians had sewn strips of adhesive tape together, back to back, sticky side out. Two of these double strips were stuck to the bare back of the player who was to carry the hidden ball. Two more double strips were stuck to the back of his sweater, on the inside.

"Late in the game, when dusk came on, the Indians had the ball. This was the play they had been waiting for. As the ball was snapped back from center, the receiver grabbed it and shoved it up under the sweater of the player who was to carry it, making sure the ball was safely stuck between the strips of adhesive tape. The ball carrier was their fastest runner. As soon as the ball was fixed in place, he started. In the fading light, the opposing team had difficulty locating the ball, for several other players were faking, as though they had it. Finally the Yale team spotted this player running for their goal line with a hump on his back. They caught on to the trick then, but it was too late to stop the Indian. He went over for a touchdown which beat mighty Yale—and made football history."

Katie wondered why the two strips of tape hadn't stuck to each other. "They probably did," Mr. Bowling explained. "But they hadn't been pressed together, so it wouldn't have been hard to pull them apart as the ball was slipped between them."

"I don't see how there was time enough to do it," Bo said, speaking from his morning's experience. "As soon as that ball is snapped, the other team swarms right over you."

His father nodded. "According to my uncle, Coach Ex said his teammates guarded against that by practicing the play over and over, until they didn't lose a fraction of a second."

"Against a poor team, I think the play would have worked, even without all that practice," was Mr. Hunt's opinion. "Provided, of course, the ball carrier was screened from the enemy by his teammates while the ball was being slipped under his jersey."

"I'd like to try it sometime, wouldn't you, Barry?" said Bo.

"You can't. You have to carry the ball in your hands or under your arm, in plain sight. That hidden-ball stuff was made illegal after that game Daddy just told you about," Mrs. Bowling said.

"That wouldn't stop Mifflin from using it," Katie said, making a face. "What I'd like to do is work it on *them.*"

"We're never going to play them again," Bo said firmly.

That's what he thought.

CHAPTER EIGHT

Bo Spends
His Birthday Money

That first evening the Hunts spent with the Bowlings was the beginning of many pleasant times together for these families. The two fathers started taking turns driving each other to the city in the mornings. This neighborly arrangement left one car always at home to carry the two mothers and the children to meetings and market and music lessons together. Several times Bo spent the night in the top bunk of Barry's double-deck bed. He became so used to Katie he actually liked having her around. Now and then he would remind his parents, "Didn't I tell you the first morning we were in this house that this was the best place we ever lived?"

"You were right," Mother always agreed. "But don't wrap your heart around Cedarville. You know Daddy's main office keeps us on the move."

Sometimes Bo would think of this at bedtime. He would look out the window with the same old wish to leave his mark here, so he would not be forgotten when he left. His hope of carving his name on the bronze football had been knocked out of him by defeat in his first game. Now he thought he'd go back to his earlier ambition of cutting his name in the bark of the big tree. Still, having once dreamed a grand dream, he hated to give it up. Each time he reached this point in his thinking he fell asleep— and woke next morning to the fun of living in Cedarville.

A large part of this fun was due to having Barry and Katie for his friends. Naturally Bo thought of them at once when he received some belated birthday money from his aunt in Montana. He ran across the street to tell Barry, "She wrote for me to spend it any way I want. Come on, let's you and Katie and me go down to the drugstore."

Since Katie was spending the day with her grand-mother, the boys went without her. First they refreshed themselves at Tom Ryan's soda fountain. Then with sci-entific zeal they tested all the newest kinds of candy bars on display, comparing them with old favorites for size, flavor and chewiness. With bulging jaws and several dol-lars still in his pocket, Bo turned to other departments of the store, looking for new excitement.

It was Barry who discovered the first aid supplies.

"Katie ought to have some of these bandages for our team," he pointed out. "Just in case—"

"Sure she should!" Bo was delighted with the idea. "And adhesive tape too. We need four or five rolls of that, don't you think? And some stuff to put on cuts . . . Hey, look here! Here's something new. It's a bandage you spray on, it says on the can. For any cut or wound. We ought to have a can of this for an emergency, don't you think?"

"Let's ask Tom if it's any good," Barry suggested, starting toward the corner where the druggist was placing bottles of perfume in a showcase.

Mr. Ryan greeted them with, "I hear you lost your game with Mifflin. And that it wasn't all your own fault."

Bo was about to ask where he had heard this news, when Tom noticed the package in Bo's hand and asked if the boys were interested in first aid supplies. On learning their plan, he declared he would give them a cut rate on tape and bandages. "Yes, sir! I'm always glad to help out a football team," he said as he reached into a drawer for a booklet which he handed them. "There's something I'll throw in for nothing. It's a little book written by a famous athletic trainer. It may be of some help to Katie in taking care of you fellows' bumps and bruises."

After purchasing enough supplies to stock Katie's

wagon, Bo had over a dollar left. "You ought to spend it on yourself," Barry said.

They roamed the store looking for something which Bo might take a fancy to . . . Comics? He was tired of them . . . Pencils which wrote red, green and blue? He already had one . . . A can of stuff to spray around a room to make it smell good? Bo, who was especially fond of pleasant odors, took a sample sniff and was about to buy, when his glance strayed farther along the counter to a pink-and-green package labeled Bubble Bath. There was a picture of a tub foaming with bubbles like a strawberry soda. "Look!" he said to Barry. "Wouldn't it be fun to sit in that stuff and splash around. I believe I'll take this."

At first Barry did not think much of Bo's selection. When Mr. Ryan said there was a choice of rose or geranium, Barry groaned, "Oh, no. Not rose!" But after looking at the picture again, he too began to imagine the tickling joy of sinking to his chin in all that froth. He became still more enthusiastic when Bo said, "We could have a bubble fight!"

After Mr. Ryan put the package of bubble bath into the shopping bag with the other purchases, Bo set out for home broke and happy. As he and Barry passed the library, he said, "Let's stop in and see the bronze football."

In they went. Barry, who knew his way around, went straight to a glass case on the wall between two windows. "There it is," he said. Against a background of black velvet the trophy gleamed like some royal relic from the days of knighthood. "As long as there are any kids in Cedarville at all, I suppose they'll be coming here to read the names on this football."

"I wish we could get our names on it, don't you?"

"Maybe we will," Barry said.

"Maybe *you* will," Bo said soberly. "I'll be gone from here before I even start in high school."

Barry pointed to the words on the base of the trophy. "You don't absolutely have to be a high school player to get your name on this. See, it says, 'the boy who best carries on the football tradition.' That means younger boys have a chance."

"I know," Bo said. "But what have I done for football so far? I got licked in the only game I played."

"That wasn't our fault," Barry said. He started for the door muttering, "Everybody knows Mifflin didn't play fair. Even Mr. Ryan—"

Bo wasn't quite ready to go. He stayed behind for a moment in front of the shining trophy. Yes, here was the place for a boy to carve his name. How much better to be remembered for smashing touchdowns and for team spirit than for gashes cut into a tree! And since he probably would not stay long enough in Cedarville to put HAROLD BOWLING on the bronze football, what then? Then— he made his decision with chin lifted and shoulders squared—he would do everything he could to help Barry or one of the other boys to win that place someday. He would keep the team together now, drilling and practicing so they could move right into positions on the high school team when the time came. In that way one or two of them would certainly win the trophy. In this brave plan Bo had only one small hope for himself. He hoped that when his friends became champions they would remember him as first of all a good team man. *Maybe the way to keep from being forgotten is to help friends,* he thought as he hurried to catch up with Barry.

"Why don't you come over to our house for dinner," Barry suggested as they walked toward home.

"No, you come to my house," said Bo. "I ate at your house the last two times. I don't want to wear out my welcome. Your mother will get tired of having me around."

"No, she won't," Barry said. "Besides Katie is at Grandmother's. Mother will be glad not to have an empty place at the table."

"No, you eat at our house tonight. Mother said we are going to have roast pork and sweet potatoes," Bo insisted.

"First, we'll have dinner, then we'll take a bubble bath."

That's the way it was settled. When the boys finally came out of the bathroom, still with a few bubbles in their ears, Mr. Bowling sniffed several times and remarked that he would have mistaken them for rosebuds if he hadn't recognized their shirts. Mrs. Bowling said, "Don't tease them, Daddy. I think they smell beautiful. In fact, it's a shame to keep all this fragrance to ourselves. Let's take the boys with us and drive over to Mifflin to return the cake pan I borrowed from Lila Sanders."

"Not Rodney's mother!" Barry blurted before he realized he was being impolite. Bo frowned at him to keep him quiet, hoping the subject would be dropped. Unfortunately Mr. Bowling thought his wife's idea a good one. Before the boys could think of a good reason why they should be left at home, they were in the back seat of the car, headed for a visit with the last person in the world they wanted to see.

"Maybe he won't be home," Barry murmured after a mile of silence.

"He will be." Bo spoke from experience. "He's always where you don't want him."

As if to prove this, Rodney strolled across the lawn to greet them the moment Mr. Bowling stopped the car. "Well, if it isn't the Cedarville push-overs," he said, after

making quite a show of assisting Mrs. Bowling from the car and shaking hands with Mr. Bowling. "You fellows came back, I suppose, to arrange another game with my team."

"Not us!" said Barry.

"Once was enough," Bo added with his whole heart.

"Your defeat still rankles, eh?" Rodney gave them that silent stare of his. In the middle of it his nose started to twitch. He stepped nearer and took a deep breath, then came as close to showing interest as he ever permitted himself. "Well, what-do-you-know! Perfume! No wonder you can't play football. You're too dainty for such a rough game."

That did it! Even while Bo was reminding himself to calm down before he spoke, lest his tongue trick him again into trouble with Rodney, he heard a direct challenge coming from Barry.

"We'll show you how we can play football! We'll beat you any day in the week, and we won't have to cheat to do it, either." That was Barry. What could Bo do but join in? Besides, no boy worth his socks would stand for what Rodney had just said.

Rodney, having forced the other two into demanding a return game, now made them settle on a date which would give his team the advantage. Bo and Barry knew very well what they were getting into, but what else could they do?

"There wasn't any other way for us," Bo muttered on the way home.

"I know. After he said what he did, we had to play them again," Barry answered. Then, after a long pause, "Do you think we can beat them this time?"

"We'd better!" said Bo. "Now that we're into it, I'm glad we're going to get another crack at them."

Barry felt the same. So did the rest of the team when they heard. As for Mr. Mac, he was in high spirits at the news. He clapped Bo on the back and declared, "Boys, this is the best thing that could happen to you. Playing Mifflin again is the only way to take the scent of that defeat out of your nostrils."

Bo and Barry glanced at each other uneasily at the word "scent." Mac went on, "Two weeks will give us some time to get ready for them. Where's the game to be played? It ought to be in Cedarville this time."

"Whereabouts?" Barry asked. "There is only the high school field, and it is kept strictly for high school games."

"Somebody ought to fix up that old field down by the river," Bo said.

Mac nodded. "It would be a fine thing for the kids of this town if somebody did. I've often said all it would take is for one group—Boosters or PTA's or some other—to start the ball rolling." He had turned back to an electronic switch he was adjusting. A moment later he looked up at the boys. "I know who'll be glad you're going to play Mifflin again. Coach Teneyes. I must get word to him."

"We could tell him for you," Bo said quickly.

"Oh-oh, trying to find out who he is, are you?" Mac laughed to himself. "You'll just have to keep on guessing —until Coach himself is ready to let the cat out of the bag."

The boys grumbled to themselves on the way home about their unseen coach. Although they admitted they probably learned more football from his written instructions than Mifflin did from the high school boy who coached them, Bo still complained to his father that evening. "What good is a coach you can't see?"

"What good is Santa Claus?" Dad came back at him. "When you were little, you believed in Santa, didn't you? Although you didn't see him, he never failed you, did he?"

"No—but that was different."

"Don't be too sure," Dad said, turning back to his newspaper.

Next afternoon when Bo went around by the inventor's shop, there was Nantaquas with a message from Coach

Teneyes. *If you boys want to win this next game, you'll have to be a little quicker getting the ball into play. When center bends over to snap the ball back, the quarterback should keep pushing his hands in under. Quarterback has hands cupped together, fingers spread apart, and the instant they feel the ball, he pulls it toward him and holds it with all three hands. The third hand is his stomach.* "I must show this to Barry right away. And to our center too," Bo said to himself as he read.

Speed up on catching or intercepting long passes too. Watch the passer. Get your feet moving as he lifts the ball, and KEEP MOVING—eyes on the ball, following it. Figure out where you'll be able to pull the ball out of the air, and run for that spot. If your own team is doing the passing, be sure to give your pass receiver plenty of protection. Block all enemy players who come near him.

Many coaches say the team with the best blockers wins the game. So let's work hard on our blocking. Like this:

When Bo had read this far, he hurried to get Katie to help make copies of these instructions. Later he passed them out to his team when they met under the tackling-dummy tree. The part about blocking they read to one another so many times that he knew it by heart. He repeated it to his father at dinner.

"When the enemy has the ball, blocking begins even

before the ball is snapped. When you're down there on the line of scrimmage, you must watch the man across from you. Don't look out at the enemy backs, expecting them to give a clue to which way the play will go. If you're a lineman, you must keep your eyes on the man across from you. Do what he does. If he moves to the right or left, you move too, so that you are still face to face with him. When he starts to run, you run with him—and stop him as soon as you can. That's what our coach says, Dad. How does it sound to you?" Bo asked, proud of his performance.

"I thought you boys didn't want any opinions from old, broken-down ex-football-playing fathers," Dad said.

"Now, Daddy—" Mother smiled at him. "I think Harold's coach knows what he is talking about."

"Sure he does," Dad agreed. "But does Harold know what *he's* talking about? I mean, son, you've shown you can remember the instructions. But in a game, will you remember to *do* all that?"

"I don't have to," Bo answered with a wide grin. "That stuff is for the men in the line. I play in the backfield, you know."

"Yes, I know." Dad smiled. "You caught me that time."

Then Bo said, "There's something else I wish our coach would tell us. And that's how we can keep Mifflin from cheating."

120

"I'd suggest that you get a fair referee, who knows the rules," Dad said.

The whole Cedarville team tried to find a referee for the coming game, but with no success. Any fathers who knew football—such as Bo's and Barry's—had business to take care of on Saturday mornings. All Mr. Mac knew about football, as he himself said, was "how not to tackle a wooden Indian." Bo even went to Ryan's Pharmacy to ask if Tom would help.

"I'm afraid I can't get away from the store that long," the druggist said. "Not even if the game were being played closer home." He suddenly cocked his head and asked, "Isn't this a return game you are playing with Mifflin? Then why aren't they coming *here* to play this time?"

"Because there isn't any football field here," Bo said. "Not for younger kids to play on."

"That's true." Tom gave him a thoughtful look. "Something ought to be done about it."

"Mr. Mac says it wouldn't cost an awful lot to fix up the one at the old recreation park," said Bo.

Tom shook his head. "I'm not so sure about that. The fellows quit playing there a couple of years ago. It's down in the bottomland along the river, you see. When the fall rains come, the place is ankle-deep in mud. Players can't pull their feet loose to run with the ball . . . Still, if Mac says it could be fixed up, he knows what he's talking about. That guy can fix anything. Yes, sir. *Anything.* Why, only the other day my big ice box there conked out on me. Right in the middle of a Sunday afternoon with better than fifty gallons of ice cream ready to turn to soup. And the refrigerator people saying they couldn't get me a service man before nine o'clock at least. Then in walks Mac for a can of tobacco. In ten minutes—yes, sir—ten minutes, he finds the trouble and has that box purring again good as new."

Bo thought of all that ice cream saved. "Golly day, Mr. Mac sure is a big help to this town."

"Cedarville couldn't get along without him," Tom said. "I'm not the only businessman around here he's pulled out of a hole. He's got lots of friends among the big factory owners over in the city too. Yes, sir, Mac sure is a wizard with machines."

The druggist rang up a sale on the cash register, handed the customer her change, and turned back to Bo. "So Mac thinks the old football field could be put to use again, does he? . . . Does he have any ideas about where the money is coming from?"

"I remember he said maybe the Boosters Club, or the PTA, or—"

Tom's attention was taken by another customer. Bo started home, having failed so far to find a referee for the game. The other boys were no more successful. The best they could do was to ask Bo's mother to keep time once more. "At least we'll have one official we can depend on for fair play," they said, taking some comfort in this thought.

CHAPTER NINE

Another Game,
Another Disaster

Once again Mrs. Bowling drove a car full of boys to Mifflin. Once again Katie went in Mac's truck with Scrubby and her cart. The little wagon seemed as important as a field hospital to her now that it was stocked with the tape, bandages and supplies Bo and Barry had bought. Who would blame her for almost hoping one of the players might be injured on the field of battle? Not badly hurt, of course—perhaps just a pulled muscle for her to tape, or a cut for her to bandage according to the instructions she had studied in the *Handbook for Athletic Trainers*. She hoped some of her school friends, or at least the sisters of the other players, would be at the game to see her in her glory, but no Cedarville rooters showed up. Mifflin, however, had quite a cheering section, including the players' mothers, sisters, and brothers. This was too bad, as Bo said.

It gave Rodney the opportunity to point out once more that Cedarville was completely lacking in football spirit.

Once again the high school boy who coached Mifflin came forward to act as referee for the game. He tossed the coin. Barry won and chose to receive. "That way we'll start out getting the ball," he said to his teammates as they trotted onto the field. "Maybe we can go with it."

On their first play Barry showed how much speed he had gained in the last two weeks of practice. He dug the ball out from under the center and shoveled a short pass to Bob Harper before Mifflin got moving. The only trouble was that Jack Pancake, the left halfback, had gone to the wrong side of the line, causing Bo to pivot into him on his way to run interference for Bob. Tall, tangle-footed Jack brought down both himself and Bo. A Mifflin tackler stopped Harper after no gain. Bo picked himself up with a sigh. Since Cedarville had only eleven men, there was no one to substitute for Jack. Bo decided to keep him from messing up any more of their plays by getting Barry to assign Jack to take care of the end on that side of the line. "See that lanky guy?" Bo pointed out the end to Jack. "On every play, you are to stop him. Don't pay any attention to anyone else. Just follow him and block him, no matter where he goes or what he's trying to do."

From then on Bo felt he had to back for both himself

and Jack. This kept him so busy he didn't see the trouble in the line until Ned Krutsky, right guard, stormed out of a pile-up claiming Mifflin had been offsides and the referee didn't call a penalty. Other Cedarville players, who also thought the referee unfair, were shouting angrily, "If they want to play crooked, we'll do the same." There was a lot of stamping and throwing of helmets to the ground. Bo muttered to Barry and Bob, who were closest to him, "You'd never catch Scotty Freeman acting like this, I'll bet."

"I'll bet Scotty never played a team like Mifflin," Bob snapped. "The only way to handle them is to give them a dose of their own medicine."

Bo did not agree. Scotty's words echoed in his mind. *Walk your straightest. Fight your hardest. And win—or lose—by the rules.*

"I still think we can beat 'em fair and square," Bo said to his team. "Come on. Let's try old 33."

The boys spread out to receive Barry's pass, but of the three, only Bo managed to sidestep his blockers and be free to catch. Since he was the farthest away, this made a long throw for Barry. Bo did all he could to help by running forward to meet the ball as it came down. *Plunk!* Right into his hands! He clamped it tight to his ribs and started to run. He was close to the edge of the field, as far from on-coming enemy tacklers as possible. Realizing the danger of his position, he was very careful not to step outside the boundary line. Suddenly, to his surprise, he saw beneath his feet the cross-striped end zone. He had made a touchdown!

Immediately several Mifflin players claimed he had stepped out of bounds as he ran. He knew he had not. The referee wouldn't listen to him. The ball was taken back and put in play on Mifflin's seventy-six yard line. Two plays later, Mifflin took the ball and went for a touchdown. Cedarville took what small satisfaction it could from blocking the kick for the extra point.

The score still stood 6–0 for Mifflin when the timekeeper called the end of the first half. Bo and his teammates dragged across the field to their bench. Scrubby passed cups of water. "Katie says you mustn't drink it. Just squish it around in your mouth, then spit it out."

Katie nodded. "The book says not to drink when you're panting." She was hopping mad at Mifflin's unsportsmanlike conduct. She, and many of the players as well, repeated Bob's words about wanting to give Mifflin a dose of its own medicine. Bo said, "No," very firmly, even though he felt he had been cheated out of his touchdown.

"Any time you change your mind," Katie said to him, "I have the stuff ready for you."

"What stuff?" They all were curious.

"This." She showed them several loosely rolled objects which she took from a compartment in her water cart. They were strips of wide adhesive tape sewed back to back. "I used the needle and thread I brought along to sew up your jerseys when you tear them," she explained. "I sewed these strips so we could work the hidden ball play."

"The hidden ball play?" Bo remembered the night his father told them how that trick once had been worked in a real game. He also thought of the time his team had tried it in practice, just for fun. "Katie, we can't use that play now. It's against the rules."

"*They* don't care about the rules," she answered. "Why should *we?*" The rest of the boys agreed with her. Scrubby echoed, "Why should *we?*"

Even Bo began to weaken as he thought of the way Mifflin had gypped him out of his touchdown. Still he insisted, "The rules *are* football. If we don't stick to the rules, we're not really playing football. Then we wouldn't deserve to call ourselves a *football* team."

Katie shrugged. "If you change your mind," she repeated, "I have the stuff ready for you."

Early in the second half, Mifflin made a first down by the same unfair trick they had used to win their first game with Cedarville. On the next play, they walked over discouraged Cedarville for a touchdown. Barry, as captain, protested to the referee that when a ball carrier has made a "three-point landing" he is not allowed to rise from his knees and go forward to gain more yards. "That used to be allowed," Barry said politely, "but the rules have been changed."

"Once a rule, always a rule," decided the referee. Thus he stopped all argument. Again there was nothing Cedarville players could do except block the kick. "Unless we use a few out-of-date rules ourselves," some of them said. "The referee wouldn't dare penalize us for that. Not after what he just said."

Katie had the same thought. At the end of the third quarter she pulled her cart onto the field and handed the boys the sewed-together tapes. "Better use this," said she.

Although Bo still was not in favor of the idea, he helped Katie smooth the tape on Barry's bare back and on the inside of his jersey. Barry, being the smallest and fastest, was the best player for the trick play. "You keep an eye on the referee," Katie said to Scrubby as they worked. "Don't let him find out what we're doing."

The referee at that point must have noticed some unusual activity among the Cedarville players. He started toward them to investigate. Scrubby headed him off by running to the other side of the field as if to attack the entire Mifflin team with his two small fists.

Cedarville went into the last quarter with more confidence, now that they had a trick up their sleeve. Or rather, up Barry's jersey. "Let's don't use it unless we absolutely have to," were Bo's final instructions. "And you, Barry, quit scratching your back or you'll give the whole thing away."

With Mifflin having 12 points to Cedarville's none, the boys decided their only hope (unless they used the illegal play) was to try Number 33 every chance they had. Presently Mifflin kicked out of a bad spot, Johnny Nelson caught the ball and reached the forty-yard line before he was stopped. Cedarville didn't waste any time in the huddle. "Hut!" The ball was snapped and they started old 33.

As Barry took the ball and began stepping back, Bo had one of those spur-of-the-moment ideas which a born player sometimes has. Before heading out beyond the Mifflin blockers, he first made a few steps toward Barry as if expecting to be handed the ball. This slight change threw off the Mifflin end who was coming across to tackle Barry. (He came so quickly that Bo, thinking it over later, decided the end must have broken the rules and started across the scrimmage line before the ball was snapped.)

As the Mifflin player hesitated, wondering whether to tackle Barry or Bo, Barry had time to dodge him and get away to the side. Bo whirled and ran across into enemy territory. Watching out of the tail of his eye, he saw Bob Harper cross behind him. Then, up ahead, Nick Nelson crossed his path with a Mifflin man at his heels. Bo heard a runner coming behind him and side-stepped. But there were two runners. As he avoided one, the other brought him down. He thought as he hit the ground, *I hope Bob is free to catch Barry's pass.*

Bob caught it on the run, and kept on going. Mifflin had been so sure they had stopped the pass by blocking Bo and Nick that they hadn't noticed Bob slip over to receive. Now he was trucking toward the goal line with nobody near him except a Mifflin end, far behind, who had been blocked by Jack Pancake and broken away. Barry kicked the point after touchdown, giving his team seven points to Mifflin's 12.

"Another touchdown will beat them!" The words roared along Cedarville's line. Let's go! We'll pour it on fast!"

Time was running out now. Mifflin lost its head at the thought of a possible defeat and seemed to forget the rules completely, until the referee even had to call penalties. Bo held his team steady, although tempers were mounting on both sides to the point where Mifflin players started calling names across the line of scrimmage.

Cedarville linemen would not stand for this. They rammed into their opponents fiercely enough to knock the name-calling back into their throats. Then the Mifflin backfield took it up. Bo heard his own name . . . "Yoo-hoo, Bowling Ball! Are you round and hard and got three holes in your head? . . . Yoo-hoo, Bowling Ball!"

"How much more are we going to take from them?" Dick Maull at center flung over his shoulder at his teammates. Barry wanted to call the hidden ball play but Bo said, "Not yet." He was determined to keep his head—even if eleven Mifflin men were screaming that it had holes in it.

Then Mifflin started on Jack . . . "Yoo-hoo, Pancake! Oh, Pancake! Are you brown on the bottom and ready to flip?" . . . The chant was repeated over and over . . . "Yoo-hoo, Pancake!"

Bo was furious. He may once have been amused by some of Cedarville's odd names, but that was far different from the ridicule being shouted at Jack. Now even the Mifflin rooters took it up. "Yoo-hoo, Pancake!"

Bo made his decision. His team had taken enough abuse. They would take no more, not even for the sake of the game itself.

There was no question about Cedarville's next play. They had the ball on the third down. For safety's sake they should kick. But who cared about protecting a losing score with the whole team muttering, "Let's *ruin* them!" and Scrubby squealing from the sidelines, "Kill 'em!"?

The team wasted no time in the huddle. Barry already had pulled out the tail of his jersey and was reaching underneath to separate the sticky strips of tape. The boys lined up. Bo took a deep breath to keep his hands from shaking. He was the one who must receive the ball from the snapper-back. If he fumbled, the play was lost, and along with it Cedarville's last chance to even scores with the enemy.

"Hut!" Bo felt the ball sting his hands. Barry was already beside him with Bob jerking up the back of his flapping jersey. Bo slammed the ball against Barry's back. He and Bob gave a couple of quick slaps at the tape as they pulled down the shirt. Barry was on his way, with Bob running interference.

The Cedarville line, having held like a stone wall during this important operation, now started to crack. Mifflin linemen were trickling through. Mifflin backs, who were deep in their own territory expecting a kick, realized their mistake. Led by Rodney Sanders, they galloped in to bring down the ball carrier. Rodney gave no more than a glance at Barry and Bob passing by with hands empty and arms pumping. He went for the knot of Cedarville players from which Bo now spurted, hunching one shoulder and attempting to run in two directions at once. To an experienced eye such as Rodney's, these signs plainly marked a player who couldn't make up his mind whether to run with the ball or throw it.

There was no indecision about Rodney. He lunged at Bo's legs, whirled him to the ground, and held him pinned with both arms. He was driving in his knee when he discovered Bo did not have the ball. At that moment three more Mifflin men piled on. *This is against the rules too,* Bo thought. *I'm glad we tricked 'em . . . I hope Barry makes it.*

Suddenly Rodney and his teammates stopped pummeling Bo and peeled off as fast as they had piled on. He sat up but his legs weren't quite ready to stand. He saw a hubbub around Mifflin's goal posts which told him Barry had arrived with the ball. But there were no cheers. Not even from Scrubby and Katie. The only sound he heard was an anxious call from the timekeeper. "Are you all right, Harold?"

"Sure I am!" He waved to his mother to prove it as he crawled to his feet and started for the goal to line up with his team for the try for point-after-touchdown.

"Boo-oo-oo! Boo-oo-oo!" All at once the Mifflin crowd found their voices and protested the touchdown. "Cheaters!" they howled. *"Cheaters!"*

"It's against the rules!" the referee shouted and pounded his fist. "It's against the rules!"

"The Carlisle Indians once used the same play," Bo told him. Bo's teammates and the timekeeper backed him up.

"That was a long time ago," the referee argued. "You can't expect to—"

"You've been using some rules that were declared illegal a long time ago too," Mrs. Bowling said quietly. "And you claimed the touchdowns made by those rules. Why can't Cedarville claim this touchdown? . . . There are exactly ten seconds left to play. Does Mifflin wish to finish the game or quit now?"

Either way, Mifflin was bound to lose. They chose to play out the ten seconds, running back the kick-off and gaining a couple of yards on the final down. They left the field so mad they wouldn't even speak to their referee. Rodney was in such a bad temper he hurried his mother away in spite of her protests that she wanted to talk to Madge Bowling.

The 13–12 victory brought little joy to the Cedarville boys. The cry of "Cheaters!" followed them from the field and took all the fun out of football.

The Editor
Hears the Story

"Cheaters!" After Bo went to bed that night he still could hear the Mifflin players shrieking, "We'll never forget this! . . . Cheaters!"

He had made a name for himself, all right. It was not the kind of name he wanted. As he rolled and tossed, he could see in the moonlight the tree outside his window. "Stand your straightest," it seemed to remind him in Scotty Freeman's words. "And win or lose by the rules . . . win or lose by the rules . . . by the rules . . . the rules." He drifted into sleep sighing, "I suppose we'll have to play them again . . . by the rules."

"Of course you'll have to play them again," Mac said the next afternoon when Bo and Barry found him in his shop and told him the whole story of their game with Mifflin. "And we'll take care to have some officials who know their business, so there'll be no illegal shenanigans. Once and for all—or at least for this season—we'll settle the question of which is the better team. The *Two-Village Times* can announce the winner, and that will end the bickering."

The mention of the community newspaper brought an unpleasant thought to Bo's mind. "I suppose Rodney has already told the *Times* that we—" he choked a little on the word, "—cheated to win. And they'll print whatever he tells them about us."

"You have a right to tell the editor your side, you know," Mac said.

"Do you think he would listen to us?" Barry asked.

"Sure." Mac nodded. "A good newspaperman always wants to hear both sides of a story. I'll take you to see him myself. His plant is just a couple of blocks from here. I go over there two, three times a month to doctor that old linotype machine he's got."

By this time Katie, who was practicing her music lesson when Barry left home, now caught up with the boys. After a quick glance to make sure her first aid cart was safe in its proper corner of the shop, she was ready to go with the others to call upon the owner and editor of the *Two-Village Times.*

"Hi, Mac," the editor barked as they entered a tiny

office where stacks of newspapers spilled from the cluttered table to the floor, and the wastebasket overflowed around the big desk. "What have you got here, Mac?"

"Rand, I want you to listen to these kids' story," Mac said, giving the boys a nod.

In the face of the editor's fierce scowl, Barry became suddenly timid and Bo found himself talking about the "bidden hall" play and "breams that roke the tules." It was a good thing Katie was there. Nobody could frown at Katie for long. In a few minutes the editor was smiling at her explanation, agreeing the rules had been broken by both sides, and—at a suggestion from Mac—promising to "kill" the report which Rodney Sanders already had telephoned in for the Mifflin team.

"I knew he'd do that," Bo said, calmer now and speaking quite distinctly. "We want to play Mifflin once more, with fair refereeing and—"

"And on your own field this time," the editor put in.

This brought up the old problem again. Cedarville had no field.

"We've got to have one," Bo said, trying to think how the old gridiron could be put into shape for a game. "I noticed somebody mowed the grass there—"

"State highway department," the editor told him. "Trying out new weed-cutting equipment."

"Now we don't have to worry how to get it cut," Bo went on. "We boys could mark it off with that tennis court marker I saw in your shop, couldn't we, Mr. Mac?"

"Sure. I'll mix you up a batch of whitewash any time you want it," Mac promised. "But what are you going to do for goal posts?"

"That's got me stumped too," Bo said.

"Those old wooden ones are all rotted to pieces. I don't think we could use any part of them," Barry added.

Bo had an idea. "Say! How about pipe? Gas pipe. I saw a lot of it in front of the second-hand store next to your place—" he looked at Mac. "Why couldn't we buy some of that to make goal posts with?"

Mac glanced over the children's heads and said to the editor, "Rand, you know how dead set I am against helping people who don't help themselves. But when this boy here has figured out how to make that old gridiron usable, I think grownups should pitch in with some assistance, don't you?"

"I do, Mac. I do indeed." The editor nodded several times, jumped up, sat down again, and began to rummage in his desk drawer, still talking. "As far as gas pipe is concerned . . . I've printed a lot of handbills and run a lot of ads for that second-hand store fellow. He never paid me a cent but he did give me a due bill . . . It's around here

140

somewhere . . . I'll never use it to buy anything in that junk heap he runs . . . Where is that thing? . . . So you kids may as well have it to buy pipe to make your goal posts . . . Ah! At last!" He fished up a piece of paper, unfolded it, looked at it and handed it to Bo. "Here you are. I'll sign it and it will pay for all the pipe you need."

The boys and Katie were so sincere in their thanks that he smiled again, adding, "If there is anything else I can do to help, just tell me." He jumped up again, ran his fingers through his hair, sat on the edge of his desk, tapped the floor with his foot, and suggested, "I have a print shop here, you know. Would you like us to run off some tickets to sell to your game?"

Sell tickets? Bo and Barry looked at each other. "Who would pay to see us play?" they asked.

"The world is full of folks who'll pay to see any kind of a contest." The editor drummed on the desk with his fingers. "I just thought—"

"We could make this a real contest!" Bo interrupted, carried away with another idea. "The big final championship game between Cedarville and Mifflin! And we *could* sell tickets. The Mifflin crew could sell them too. They could keep the money they make, and we could use the money we make to fix up the field, so we'll have a good place to play next year."

"It would need to be drained, first of all," Mac said. "That takes money. How much do you figure on charging for these tickets?"

Everybody looked at everybody else. Finally someone said, "Twenty-five cents." There were nods of agreement all around. Mac added, "And one dollar for adults."

"Do you think many adults will come?" Katie asked, as if she were already counting dollars.

"They won't want to pay that much." Her brother gave his opinion.

"Don't be so all-fired sure," Mac said with a large wink. "You heard what the editor said. We've got the makings of a real contest in this thing. All we need do is spread the word around, sell those tickets—and keep our fingers crossed that we'll have dry weather for the game. Because if there comes a hard rain, that field will turn to a swamp. The players will get so covered with mud they won't be able to recognize their own teammates. And as for you, Katie—" Mac waggled a finger at her, "—you won't be able to pull your Nightingale wagon away from the sidelines."

"Nightingale wagon? What's that?" The editor reached for a piece of paper and took the black pencil from behind his ear. "There's a story for the *Times* in this somewhere. Now, young lady, suppose you tell me—"

142

He made a few notes as Katie talked; then he said he'd send his photographer to take a picture of her with her water cart. "Better have a couple of Cedarville players in the picture, and you putting a bandage on one of them," he added. "Thanks for bringing these kids in, Mac. This will make a good front-page feature."

"There's another good story for you in this team," Mac said with a quiet chuckle. "Would you like to see a picture of the fellow they get instructions from?"

"Is he so unusual?" the editor asked with a frown.

"Take a look and see what you think." Mac took from his wallet a yellowed newspaper clipping and showed it to his friend. Bo, being closest to the editor, looked over his shoulder thinking this was their chance to find out who their coach was.

"Why, that's the wooden Indian in front of your shop, Mac! Who are you trying to fool?"

The inventor put the clipping back in his wallet, still laughing to himself. "All I said, Rand, was 'There's another good story in this team.' You take care of these kids right, and we'll tell you all about it later."

With that, Mac led the three young people out of the office, stopping just long enough to arrange with the editor about the printing of the tickets "as soon as we settle on the date for the game."

Settle on a date for the game? Bo suddenly realized he would have to meet and talk with Rodney, for Barry said, "You made the arrangements the other times, so you're the one to do it again, I think. Especially since you know their captain better than any of us."

"Decide the date as soon as you can, Bo," Katie said. "So we can get the tickets printed and have more time to sell them."

Bo thought, *I can't face Rodney. I don't want to see him or talk to him as long as I live.* He could still hear Rodney calling him, "Cheater!" Then another thought came to him. Here was a chance to change that shameful name which he and his teammates had made for themselves. Here was their chance to start over, to wipe out their bad record and to become known as a team which carried on the football tradition Scott Freeman had set in Cedarville. "I'll talk to Rodney tonight," Bo promised before his good intentions could desert him.

Making that telephone call was one of the hardest things Bo ever did. "Hi, Rodney," he said when the other boy answered. "This is Bo."

"Oh, hello, Cheater," Rodney said.

"Same to you," Bo retorted, more to keep his spirits up than in actual anger. Then, being very careful not to twist his words in his excitement, he opened the subject of a

144

third, or play-off, game between Mifflin and Cedarville.

Rodney was not interested. Bo could feel his blank stare coming through the phone with the words, "You guys would only cheat again."

Bo began to wonder what he would do if Rodney refused to play. He tried to make his proposition sound as attractive as possible. "We'll make a regular championship game of it. We'll have a real referee this time. Maybe an umpire too."

"We beat you once. Why should we do it again with a different referee?" Rodney sounded ready to hang up.

Bo quickly mentioned selling tickets. As a last hope to persuade Rodney, he said, "You Mifflin boys can have the money for all you sell."

"We could sell three times as many as you," Rodney boasted at once.

"Bet you can't." Bo held his breath. Would Rodney take this bait?

Rodney swallowed it whole. "We'll just show you who can sell the most tickets," he said.

After that, Bo easily got him to agree on a date. They chose a Saturday in November when State U would be playing far away and Scott Freeman's home-town fans, being unable to watch their hero, might buy tickets for the Cedarville-Mifflin game instead.

On the next question, although Rodney did not seem enthusiastic about playing the contest in Cedarville, he gave in at once. "Thank heaven he doesn't know how muddy our field might be, or he would have backed out," Barry said when Bo told him the good news.

The next step was to send the word to the *Two-Village Times*. Bo wanted Dad to look over the notice before leaving for the city, so he worked on it next morning at the breakfast table.

"That pencil you are chewing is not very nourishing, dear," said Mother. "How about another piece of toast? And don't forget to drink your milk."

Bo stopped writing to reach for his glass of milk. The familiar words on it—Rose Bowl Game—struck him with a new meaning. *That's what our game is going to be,* he thought. *A kind of little Rose Bowl Game.* It would decide the champion of two rival teams, wouldn't it? And tickets would be sold to it. Bo said, thinking out loud, "The only difference between the Rose Bowl Game and ours is that we won't have any parade."

"And your bowl won't be so rosy either," Dad reminded him with a smile. "From what I hear around Cedarville, this field of yours is a mess after a rain."

Bo nodded absent-mindedly. "Why couldn't we have a parade?" He spoke more to himself than to his father.

"That might get more people interested in buying tickets. And the more tickets we sell, the more money we'll have to fix up the field for next year."

"But, Harold, you may not be here next year. You know the main office is always moving Daddy to someplace new," Mother said.

"At least I can help fix up the field while I *am* here, can't I?" This was all Bo said about the decision he had made a few weeks earlier. He would do everything he could to help his teammates become good football players, even if he would never have a chance at the bronze football himself.

Almost at once the game with Mifflin became The Big Thing to the Cedarville players and to Katie and Scrubby. They wanted to win with all their hearts of course, but they began to feel selling tickets was as important as a victory. As Bo pointed out to them, this was their chance to show Cedarville people how badly the boys and girls needed a recreation field. He tried to think of a good way to advertise the game. Still in his mind was the thought of the Rose Bowl Game he had seen. And the Tournament of Roses parade before the game. "Why couldn't we have a parade in connection with our game?" he asked Barry and Katie.

"Oh, let's do!" Katie's dark eyes sparkled. "We saw

the Rose Bowl parade on television. Remember, Barry? If we have one like that, I could be one of the queens in it, couldn't I?"

"We couldn't have one exactly like it, I don't suppose," said Bo, trying not to dampen her enthusiasm. "We probably couldn't have all those big floats, nor—"

"But we could have a *little* parade, couldn't we? And I could wear a Florence Nightingale costume, maybe, or a nurse's uniform. And wheel my cart. Only—" Katie always took things seriously, "—ought we call it the Rose Bowl parade? It wouldn't be, you know. And the people in California might not like us to use that name."

"Ours will be more like a mud bowl," Bo laughed.

"It will if it rains hard." Barry laughed too. Then Bo slapped him on the back, shouting, "Why not? Mud Bowl is a good name for it. That will let folks know how bad our field is."

The rest of the team laughed and agreed with Bo when he told them his idea. He hurried around to the *Times* office to see if the new name could be printed on the tickets. The editor liked it at once. "The parade is a good idea too," he said. "Now let's make sure of that date." He checked the calendar, made a note on his desk pad, and looked up at Bo. "We settled the admission price when you were here with Mac, didn't we? The next question is what kind of stock we have for tickets." He was out the door and back at his desk again before Bo knew what he meant. "You can have your tickets red, blue or light brown. The brown would kind of carry out the Mud Bowl idea, but printing doesn't show up so well on it. Same way with the blue." The editor advised, "If I were you, I'd have red tickets. They're bright and cheery and easy to find when you stick them in your wallet or purse. Okay?"

"Okay." Bo nodded, dazed at the speed with which the matter was arranged. He knew the tickets were to be printed free of charge. As he started to say thank-you, the editor threw him a wink and asked, "How about getting an interview for the *Times* with your coach about this big game?"

Bo suddenly thought *Coach Teneyes doesn't even know about the game. We must get word to him.* He stammered a hasty good-bye to the editor and hurried home by way of the inventor's shop. "Hi, Nantaquas!" He gave his usual greeting as he reached for the door-knob. Then he noticed the spindle of white paper in the Indian's head.

CHAPTER ELEVEN

Everybody
Gets in the Parade

Bo unrolled the little paper, hoping it had been left with Nantaquas by Scott Freeman. To his amazement he found this message from Coach Teneyes: *Bully for you boys for playing Mifflin again!*

"How did he know?" Bo wondered. He read on. *This time let's make it a clean game and a fair one. Don't worry about getting a referee. One will be provided for you. All you boys need do is to play your best. This means a lot of hard practice from now on . . . For one thing, do footwork drills, at recess or on the way home from school. Practice this in groups of four, each taking a turn as the leader. The leader runs, side-steps and reverses, trying to dodge the other three, who must try to stick to him like his own shadow.* As usual, the message was type-written and signed with a red crayon.

The team studied Coach's instructions and practiced them every chance they had. "He ought to be satisfied with us now," they said, feeling sure they could dodge even the swiftest Mifflin player.

But Coach Teneyes was not satisfied. Whoever he was and wherever he may have seen them, he had this word to send them: *Stop doing the duck waddle. Point your toes IN just a little and run STRAIGHT ahead. Don't simply head in the general direction of the goal line. HEAD STRAIGHT FOR THE GOAL POSTS. Chop! Chop!*

"Chop! Chop!" soon became the boys' favorite saying. "Chop! Chop!" they shouted at one another as they picked out imaginary goal posts on the way from school, running forward, pulling their knees high and propelling with their arms, as Scott Freeman once told them to do.

Along about this time Scotty was being written up in the papers as the top touchdown maker of college football. The Cedarville team sent him a telegram before an important game, saying: WE ARE WITH YOU KEEP ON MAKING TOUCHDOWNS. "That's only eight words," Bo counted as he wrote them down. "We are allowed more."

The boys added CHOP CHOP, pleased to be able to get their pet expression into the message. As Bo said, it sounded better than LOVE, which so many people put at the end of their telegrams.

With Scott Freeman doing such glorious work for football, Bo wanted more than ever for himself and his team to keep the promise to carry on the high standards Scotty had set in Cedarville athletics. His teammates felt Scotty would be satisfied if they won from Mifflin. Bo had a higher aim. He wanted to play a perfect game, to make no mistakes or fumbles, and to give every play that extra something which only a great player can give.

Before long another message from Coach Teneyes was received by Nantaquas and passed on to the team. *It is time to practice place kicking now that your goal posts are up.*

"How did he know?" the boys asked one another as they read. It was only yesterday afternoon that Bo and Barry had told their mothers they would not be home from school until late because Mac had the pipe cut and ready. Tom Ryan had said, if the boys would help, he and Mac would sneak away from business for a couple of hours and put up the goal posts. So now the slim, silvery posts stood firmly at either end of the grassy level which would soon be marked with gridiron lines. "How did Coach know the posts were up?" the boys repeated. Although they wondered for the hundredth time who their coach was and how he knew so much about team affairs, as usual they forgot their curiosity in trying to master the tasks he set for them.

Pick out your best kicker, he had written. *Let him practice at first with a long piece of tape laid on the ground, straight toward the center of the cross bar on the goal post. Let him learn his position—foot beside the tape and shoulders square with the goal posts. The trick is to take a short jab step with your right foot, then a long lunge step which brings you to three inches behind the ball. Then swing through with your right foot, and kick! Swing your arms to the front, don't let them drag behind. And after you've kicked keep on swinging your foot up, right in line with the tape, as you began.*

Everybody wanted to become a kicking specialist after reading this. The message went on to say, however, that the center and the ball holder were almost as important as the kicker. There also were instructions for the rest of the team which spread the glory around in fairly equal measure: *Your job is to protect the kicker. The line, from tackle to tackle, must make a solid wall and hold it. Let no enemy through your iron barricade until your ball holder has set up the ball behind you and the kicker has safely booted it out over your heads. The free backs and the two ends take care of any opponents who try to come around that wall on either side.*

154

As the days flew by there were more messages from Coach, and hours and hours of practice on the field and in the schoolyard. Earlier in the season Bo and Barry had held passing practice in the street after dinner. But now the days were so short the boys had trouble seeing the ball in the early darkness. However, this did not persuade them to give up football in their after-dinner hours. They merely changed from playing to selling tickets. They rang doorbells all over Cedarville. Householders expecting to be annoyed by pranksters seemed happy to buy tickets from Mud Bowl-ers instead.

"Mud Bowl is a good name for that field," chuckled a man Bo called upon one rainy night. "When we were boys, we tried to play there but had to give up. So you lads are trying to get the field drained and put in shape, are you? Well, I'll certainly give a buck toward that. Here you are, sonny."

"Thank you. And here's your ticket," Bo said. "I hope you'll come to the game."

"Not if it's weather like this!" The man laughed again. "I'd need web feet."

The whole team wished for web feet the next afternoon. As Scrubby remarked about their field, "It squids when you walk on it." When they told Mr. Mac this, he said they'd better not practice on it. "Eleven pairs of big feet could soup it up till it wouldn't be fit to play the game on."

"Suppose the field is muddy for the game? What will we do then, Mr. Mac?"

"Play anyway. It won't be half as bad for you as for the spectators."

Bo hadn't been thinking of the mud from that standpoint. What he was afraid of was that his teammates, being mostly lightweights, would slip and slide in the mud, while the heavier Mifflin boys would be able to stay on their feet. A muddy ball would be slippery, too, and a fellow was more apt to fumble it.

However, Coach Teneyes had a few words to say on this subject: *There is as much mud on the field for the other team as there is for you. The big boys are slowed to a standstill, and the little boys skid, and everybody plays with the same slippery ball and is liable to fumble. This goes for both teams, remember. So don't worry about mud.*

"All the same, *I'm* worried about it," Mac said when Bo told him this. "I've got fifty dollars worth of tycoons coming to the game, and I want 'em to enjoy it."

"Fifty dollars worth of *what?*" asked Katie, who had come to the shop with her brother and Bo to check on the supply of bandages in her cart. "What are tycoons?"

"They're big businessmen," Mac explained. "I've done a job of fixing at one time or another in nearly every manufacturing plant in the county. The owners are all friends of mine. We go fishing and duck hunting together. So, seeing as how they're sportsmen, I sold 'em tickets to the Mud Bowl Game. Felt I was doing them a favor. Three of 'em I charged a special rate of ten dollars. The other four I let in for five bucks a piece . . . As I said, that makes fifty dollars worth of tycoons coming."

"Fifty bucks for our field fund!" Barry shouted.

"Dolly gay!" Bo grew excited at the thought. "Wac, you're a monder!"

"Calm down," Mac said with a smile. "I did hope they would donate more later, after they watched you kids play, and got into the spirit of the thing. But I'm afraid that hope will go a-glimmering if those old boys have to stand around in the mud and wet."

"Why don't you invent something to keep them dry?" asked Katie, who had great faith in his powers.

"I'll certainly have to invent *something*," Mac said, scratching his head. "Just as sure as pea soup's green."

"I love pea soup," Bo said, not because that had anything to do with what they were talking about, but just because he was always interested in food. "Especially *split* pea soup," he added.

"We'll have that for our victory dinner," Barry said with a grin. "And twenty-seven different kinds of ice cream from the Purple Cow."

"Victory dinner?" Mac looked up from the screw he was turning in a disabled motor. "You're getting pretty cocky, aren't you? Talking about victory dinners before you've even played the game."

"Barry's only mocking the Mifflin team," Katie came to her brother's defense. "Their captain told Bo they were going to spend their ticket money on a big dinner when they won the game, with the favorite food of every boy on the team."

"Rodney even told me to thank our team for the dinner in advance," Bo laughed. "As if they had the game already in the bag."

"Let 'em go ahead and plan their victory dinner." Mac nodded with satisfaction. "Many a team has lost because it was over-confident."

"Rodney says they have a right to be confident. They've played together lots longer than we have. Some of them are older and bigger. And, says he—" Bo had to smile, "—they have *him* for captain and star player."

"That reminds me, Bo," said Barry. "I think you ought to be captain for this game."

"But you're the captain," Bo protested rather weakly.

"I only got shoved into it at that first game when we needed one in a hurry," Barry said. "You would make a much better captain. The other boys feel the same as I do. In fact, we're going to elect you."

Bo yearned for the honor, yet he already had another big job on his hands. "I can't neglect the parade. I'm chairman of that, you know."

"We'll all help you to get people to have floats," Barry and Katie promised. "You won't have to worry about that. Practically the whole team is on the committee anyway."

The Mud Bowl Parade was becoming quite an event in Cedarville, at least among the school children. Their principal, who had followed with interest the forming of the team and its unfortunate games with Mifflin, had praised in Assembly the boys' plans for raising a fund to put the old football field into playing condition. He must have spoken to the PTA about it also, for they voted at their November meeting to help in the cause. They also enlarged the project to include the building of a real recreation field instead of a football gridiron only. There was talk of having tennis courts, playground equipment, softball diamonds, and someday perhaps a swimming pool made by damming the river. At this point, everybody in school became enthusiastic. Girl Scouts and

159

Campfire Girls pressed their uniforms to march in the parade. Scout Troop No. 9 started hammering together a float to be propelled on six pairs of old bicycle wheels donated by the second-hand store man. The Cub Scouts took their cue from their older brothers. They wove red-white-and-blue paper in the wheels of their own bikes and hung from the cross bars signs proclaiming CEDARVILLE—Champions of the Mud Bowl.

The editor of the *Two-Village Times* ran a front-page story about the coming contest, with a picture of Katie smiling as she filled the water urn on her little cart. The following week, with mounting enthusiasm, he offered a prize of five dollars for the most original float. He printed a coupon in the paper, invited all readers to clip it, fill it out, and enter the contest. Next, Tom Ryan came forward with an offer of five dollars in merchandise from his drugstore for the most beautiful float. Even Mac began to talk of having a float in the Mud Bowl Parade.

"I'd hoist Nantaquas into my pick-up truck," he said with a sly look over his spectacles. "And in his headdress I'd fasten a banner saying LET's HANG THE INDIAN SIGN ON MIFFLIN."

Katie told him he couldn't do that because the floats all had to be little home-made ones. No trucks or automobiles were allowed.

"There will be cars to carry *us* in the parade, though," her brother said. "And the Mifflin players, too, of course."

Naturally everyone understood the teams could not be allowed to use their strength marching around town before the game. The people of Cedarville were suddenly becoming anxious about the welfare of these boys who were to uphold the community honor against outsiders. Bo was amazed to find how many doors were opened and how many heads popped out of windows to ask if he were badly hurt on the afternoon he was seen limping from practice with a bandaged knee.

"I'm all right . . . It's just a scratch," he said to left and to right. "It will heal fast. Our team trainer took care of it." As indeed she had. Katie had wanted to use some of the spray-on stuff, but decided to bandage the gash instead. A bandage looked more heroic. And if she used three times as much gauze as needed, it only served to make people more concerned about Bo's injury.

Next day Bo was back at practice, calling for "old 33." He drilled his men on this play until he could have wakened them in the middle of the night, shouted "Hut!" and they would have snapped into formation, Barry taking the ball from center, fading back while Jack Pancake braced himself to block the enemy end. Some of the boys wanted to learn a lot more plays, but Bo was following

Coach's instructions: *Number 33 can be used in several ways to surprise the enemy. When you can't use 33, give the ball to Bo and let him buck it through.* ("He must have seen me play!" Bo thrilled at this thought. "He thinks I'm good!") *The rest of the time on offense stick to your one play. On defense, make your blocks and tackles hold. You'll be able to out-fox any team which has spent its time learning a lot of different plays.*

All the same, even Bo began to question this promise the night Aunt Lila and Uncle Harry Sanders stopped in for a few minutes, bringing Rodney with them.

"I suppose it's a mistake to put these two boys together the week before their big game," Mrs. Sanders said gaily. "They'll probably sit and glower, or else chew each other to bits."

Bo's mother suggested, exactly as she had the first time Rodney had come, "Wouldn't you boys like a gingerale? Bo, there is some in the ice box."

Bo led the way, thinking of that other time. Rodney must have been thinking of it too, because he said, "I suppose you still don't have any ice cream to put in our drinks."

Bo felt much more sure of himself now than he had on his first day in Cedarville. He merely said, "No—our coach doesn't like us to eat too much sweet stuff."

162

"Your coach." Rodney gave Bo that same blank stare. "What's he got to say about it? From what I hear, you guys have never seen him."

"Who? Coach Teneyes?" Bo was stalling for time, trying to think how to put Rodney off this ticklish subject.

"If that's what he calls himself. Some friends of mine say he is really the Mifflin high school coach. And he's teaching you a lot of stuff that won't work, so we can beat you."

"Prove it!" Bo demanded.

"What for?" Rodney shrugged. "I know it's true. For one thing, the Mifflin coach's initials are T.E.—for Ted Edwards. Or for Ten Eyes."

"That still doesn't prove anything." For all he spoke so positively, Bo had a sinking feeling inside.

"Wait till you play us. You'll see then that your fine coach has really been working for our side all along," Rodney said. "We'll know ahead of time every play you run. And believe me, we'll be there to stop you." Rodney raised his eyebrows in a way which made Bo sure he knew about that one lone play of Cedarville's, especially as he went on, "My team has offensive plays and defensive plays and plays to try on the opening kick-off, and—" he broke off. "Why should I give away our strength. You'll see plenty of it when we trounce you by about—let me see—four, no, five touchdowns."

"What's all this talk about touchdowns?" Dad asked as he came into the kitchen to say, "Rodney, your mother and dad said to tell you they are leaving. They've gone out to the car."

Rodney, always polite around grown-ups, thanked him and started for the door. Behind Mr. Bowling's back, though, he held up five fingers to remind Bo of the number of touchdowns by which Cedarville would be beaten. "Cheaters," he added under his breath.

Bo winced to hear that name again. "If we are ever going to live it down," he said to himself, "we'll simply *have* to beat Mifflin." Even then, he supposed, Rodney's team would ignore that defeat and keep harping on the time Cedarville won by cheating. *It looks like we can't win either way. The joke is on us.* It was the kind of joke even Bo did not feel like laughing at.

He started his homework with his mind more on Rodney's words than on the problems in the book. "Offensive plays, defensive plays," he muttered. "Plays to try—why, Coach never said a word to us about defensive plays! Could Rodney be right about him? Is he really from Mifflin and working against us?"

Bo was more alarmed than ever next morning when Barry said on the way to school, "Guess what Dad told us at breakfast? He heard at Boosters Club meeting last night that Ted Edwards, the Mifflin high school coach, is going to referee our game."

CHAPTER TWELVE

The Mud Bowl Game

Bo and Barry no longer doubted the story that the Mifflin coach was to referee the Mud Bowl Game. They felt the arrangement especially unfair since this official was also supposed to be working against their team although he posed as their own coach. Bo stopped in Ryan's Pharmacy to discuss the matter. He knew Tom belonged to the Boosters and also was interested in the Cedarville boys' team and their big game. "Don't you think Coach Edwards might favor Mifflin, Mr. Ryan?" Bo asked, after they had talked about Edwards being a referee.

"No, no," Tom said. "Rules are rules, and you can trust any coach to follow them, even against his own team. Besides, Edwards won't be the only man officiating at the game. The Cedarville High coach will work with him. We'll see that there is a timekeeper from each side too. Yes, sir—" he clapped Bo on the shoulder as he went to

167

answer the phone, "—we've done everything we can to help you boys win a fair victory over Mifflin."

"If we do win, they'll claim we cheated just the same," Barry said when Bo told him this.

"Let's not worry about that now. We may not win!" Bo half laughed. "Those Mifflins have it on us in weight, you know."

"I know." Barry nodded. "And we don't have any defensive plays." His disappointment over this spread to the rest of the team. Coach Teneyes also must have heard about it in his own mysterious way, for he sent them a message through Nantaquas: *The best defense you can have is a good offense. Just simply don't let the enemy get the ball. If they do, tackle their ball carrier at once, and spoil every pass they attempt.*

"What do you think of that, Dad?" Bo repeated the words to his father.

"Sounds like good advice to me," Dad said. "It wouldn't do for more experienced teams of course. But it should work for you beginners, if you have practiced blocking and tackling hard enough. Have you?"

"I think so." It seemed to Bo they had practiced *very* hard. Still, you never knew how much was "enough" until the test came. In two more days he would certainly know the answer.

Those two days were so full that the boys were glad their unknown coach left word for them to go easy on the practice. *Keep your bodies strong, your minds keen and your hearts high for the game.*

Since the contest was such an important one, the team felt their coach should be with them on their bench during the game. They suggested this to Mac, who said as he had before, that Coach Teneyes would not put in an appearance. Bo asked, "Is there any reason why we can't write to him and ask him to come? We could leave the note with Nantaquas, the way he does."

Mac said, "Go ahead and write, if you want to. But I don't think he'll answer."

He didn't. But their feeling of being deserted was lessened by a telegram from Scott Freeman, sent to Mac's shop, saying: THREE CHEERS FOR THE MUD BOWL PLAY YOUR BEST IN IT.

If Scotty and Coach Teneyes were to be absent from the game, at least a great many other people in the two villages would be there to root for one side or the other. When Bo, Barry and Katie counted the ticket money in the *Times* editorial office, they had $178.25. "That's not counting Scrubby's mother and dad and his two grandfathers," Katie said. "They're coming but he hasn't collected from them yet."

"That makes $182.25. Will that be enough for the new field?" the boys asked.

The editor looked at them over his typewriter. "That's quite a respectable amount. Especially since the Boosters promised to match whatever you kids make. And the PTA voted to double it," he reminded them. "That adds up to—roughly, a little over seven hundred dollars. Quite a bit of improvement can be made on the field with that amount. And there's a possibility people who aren't interested in the game so far, will want to buy tickets when they see the parade tomorrow."

Tomorrow! Bo felt a quiver in his stomach. "Golly day, we aren't ready for the Mud Bowl Game yet."

"No!" Barry said in a hollow voice.

"One thing is ready though." Bo laughed. "The field. Mifflin can't say we cheated on the mud."

Indeed the field was living up to its name in a most extravagant manner, after three straight days of rain.

Saturday, to everyone's joy, dawned with blue skies and a true football nip in the air. Bo awoke feeling fine. The moment he remembered the game, a lot of jumping beans seemed to start leaping inside him. "Buck fever," he said sternly to himself. "Don't pay any attention to it."

After breakfast there was plenty to do to keep his mind off the game. First he went to the shoe repair shop to get his old shoes, which the shoe man had fitted with football cleats. Most of the team had this done to a pair of old shoes that week. Cleats would help prevent slipping on the muddy field, besides making the boys feel as if they had real uniforms. By this time they all had their own helmets, for safety's sake, and most had football pants. But their jerseys were of all kinds and colors.

Bo's next stop was the inventor's shop where he met Barry and Katie, who had come to get the water cart. Mr. MacGillicuddy was putting the finishing touches on what he called "an invention to keep the tycoons from foundering in the mud." For each of his special friends he had made a pair of duck feet out of plywood. These were cut in the shape of snowshoes, and fastened with a strap over the toe of the wearer's shoe and another around his ankle. "The things work too," Mac said with satisfaction. "I tried a pair over at the field yesterday. By hokey, I didn't get the least speck of mud on my shoes."

As Bo and Barry left, Mac wished them the best of luck in the game. "I'll see you at the field of course," he added. "But since I'll be one of the timekeepers, it wouldn't look right for me to seem partial to your side in front of everybody."

By the time Bo reached home, the mid-day newscast of the *Two-Village Times* was telling the radio listeners that

Mud Bowl activities would start at one o'clock, when all those in the parade, as well as members of both teams, would meet at the school. A few minutes before the hour, Bo heard Barry's familiar whistle from across the street. He went out to meet the two Hunts.

"How do I look?" Katie asked him, twirling in her blue nurse's cape until its red lining rippled and the perky blue cap slid off her short black curls.

"I think the wagon looks prettier than she does, don't you, Bo?" Barry teased. "You and I really did a good job decorating it."

They heard a door slam, then a shout, "What you *doo-oo*-ing? Wait for me!" Without this familiar greeting they never would have recognized the weird, mud-plastered figure which mounted its tricycle and came pedaling toward them. "I'm a float in the pee-rade," Scrubby announced. "Here, Katie, will you please keep the signs my mother made for me and fasten them on when the pee-rade starts?"

The editor of the newspaper and the president of the PTA, who also were judges for the parade, helped line up the floats and the different groups of marchers. Scrubby almost missed the parade entirely by being occupied at the drinking fountain when the procession started. "I have to keep my mud wet, or it comes off," he explained to

172

Katie, who ran back to get him. And a good thing she did too, for he was a smash hit with everybody. All along the line of march there were roars of laughter when this small, incredibly dirty figure wheeled into view with a sign across the handlebars: "DON'T LET THIS HAPPEN TO YOUR BOY! And another sign at the back of his saddle: CLEAN UP THE MUD BOWL! All the mothers admired the public spirit of Scrubby's mother, who would have to clean up the bathroom after him when the parade was over. All the boys envied him. And the editor, who was striding from one end of the parade to the other, whispered to Bo that Scrubby looked like a cinch to win the prize for the most original float. The prize for the most beautiful one, he said, probably would go to the Brownie Scouts who were riding their bikes in a hollow-square formation, supporting in the center a cardboard football field held up by wires fastened to their handlebars. Later the editor came by with another piece of information for Bo. "The Men's Brotherhood of the Community Church just handed us twenty-five dollars for the fund. I've never seen the people of Cedarville push anything the way they are doing with this playing field. Everybody wants to have a hand in it."

With so many other persons helping, Bo wondered if he and his part would not be quickly forgotten. "It looks like I've failed again," he decided with a small laugh at his own expense. "The only chance I have left to make a name for myself in Cedarville is to do it in this game. Make a spectacular touchdown, maybe. Or kick a winning field goal." These were his thoughts as the team rode at the end of the parade in cars, driven slowly and choking with importance, cheered by every loyal fan along the sidewalk. Among these were a group of girls from Katie's class, who had worked up a cheer of their own:

> Our team is SO sweet!
> Our team can't be beat!

For good luck each girl carried in her coat pocket a lump of sugar taken from the bowls on the tables in Shingledecker's and sealed in a paper cover printed with the name of that popular local restaurant. As Katie told Bo, whenever the girls put their hands in their pockets they felt the sugar lump and reminded one another that "our team is so sweet!"

Now these faithful rooters and many others along the line of march fell in behind the parade and followed it to the field. The teams piled out to run through their warm-up drills. Bo noticed again, with a sinking heart, how much larger Mifflin was man for man than his own team. He also knew how much more experienced they

were in playing. Furthermore he could tell they had been working hard for this game. There was something about the confident way in which they sprang to position and snapped the ball that caused him to give up all ideas of distinguishing himself in this contest with them. The most he hoped for now was to be saved from disgracing himself by poor playing. As for a victory, a small voice inside him said, "Golly day, we'll be lucky to tie the score!" But he wouldn't listen to that.

Before he was quite ready for it, the thrilling moment came when he, as Cedarville's captain, was called to meet with Rodney Sanders of the visiting team. The coin was tossed. Rodney won and decided to receive. Bo chose to defend the north goal, which gave his team the wind at their backs to help with kicks and passes. With the two high school officials looking on, he shook hands with Rodney while the *Times* photographer snapped a picture. Scrubby came running from the bench with the tee to hold the ball for the kick-off as Cedarville strung out along the forty-yard line. Bo was holding his breath from excitement till his throat ached and the blood pounded in his ears as the official called, "Ready, Mifflin?" Rodney signaled.

Now! . . . "Ready, Cedarville?"

"Let's go!" Bo croaked and raised his hand.

176

The whistle blew. He surged forward with his teammates. Sh-sh-shoom! The ball took off. He cut his speed as the linemen hurried ahead to tackle the receiver. At this time it was his job, with Jack on the other flank, to take care of the ball carrier in case he got past the forward wave of Cedarville players.

"At-a-boy, Henderson!" Bo shouted as the tackle brought the man down.

Mifflin started with the ball on its forty-yard line, tried two running plays which gained only eight yards, then decided to punt. Big Dick Maull broke through to spoil the kick. The ball zigzagged upward and sideward. Nick Nelson leaped for it and was immediately tackled. It was Cedarville's ball in the center of the field.

"Let's take it from here. Chop! Chop!" Bo said in the huddle. Although Barry was quarterback, there was little need for calling the play. The boys all knew a line buck was what they'd try here, with Bo carrying the ball. They took their stance. Dick bent over the ball, snapped it back. Barry pulled it out and slammed it at Bo, who barreled through Mifflin for three yards.

Everybody took it for granted they would repeat the buck. Bo thought this might be a mistake, but it turned out all right because the Mifflin center also expected the same play. He started too soon. "Mifflin offside," the referee declared. And back went Mifflin for a five-yard penalty.

Bo winked at Barry, who answered with a wide grin of satisfaction. This time Rodney and his team could not claim unfair officiating, for the referee who called the penalty on them was Ted Edwards, their home-town coach. Bo also realized Mr. Edwards was not working against Cedarville, which seemed to prove Rodney was wrong in claiming this official was actually Coach Teneyes.

Two plays later Edwards again penalized Mifflin for being offside. "Yah! You can't get by with that stuff with an honest referee!" the Nelson boys taunted when the ball was handed back to Cedarville for another first down. Cedarville was beginning to roll now. The players were so steamed up they felt they could ride over everything in their way.

The wiley Rodney stopped them by calling time out. The Cedarville boys lost their fire while the Mifflin team made a great show of cleaning the mud from its shoes. Jack Pancake and some of the linemen blamed Mifflin when their next play failed. "Why get mad? We learned something from them, didn't we?" Bo asked. "Besides, they gave us a chance to clean our shoes too."

The field was growing muddier with every play as

twenty-two pairs of cleats stirred the wet earth to a kind of lumpy gravy. Two plays later Bo called time out—not to stop a Mifflin drive but to let his men wipe the mud out of their eyes. Katie (who had read every page of the athletic trainers' handbook from Ryan's drugstore) came on the field with an armload of towels which she had stowed in her cart for just this purpose. "The mud really flies when those big tackles plough through it," her brother said, thanking her for a towel.

As Coach Teneyes once told them, "There's as much mud on the field for the other team as for you." Presently Mifflin, too, called for time to wipe faces and hands. Even the officials tucked towels in their belts to clean the ball between plays. By the time the quarter ended, with no score on either side, both players and spectators looked soggy and mud-spattered. The only clean shoes to be seen were on Mr. Mac's tycoons, who clomped up and down the sidelines on their plywood duck feet, enjoying every minute.

So far, the teams had been feeling each other out and getting accustomed to the mud. Furthermore, the presence of two teacher-officials, the excitement of the parade, and the atmosphere of a big-time championship contest, all had a disturbing effect on the boys. "They play," one of the tycoons remarked, "as if they're in dancing class."

With the start of the second period, however, the boys began to look more like seasoned players. Bo was the first to let himself go with a great smashing block which earned a rousing cheer from the Cedarville crowd. Across the line of scrimmage Rodney, not to be outdone, stepped back with the ball and heaved a well-aimed pass for a gain of eight yards on the next play. By this time his team no longer was trying to win by unfair means. With good refereeing, Mifflin had settled down to playing by the rules, and had won the respect of its opponents.

CHAPTER THIRTEEN

Hero for a Week

"Here we go for a touchdown, a touchdown, a touch-down!" chanted the Mifflin fans. *"Here we go—"*

A fumble! Ned Krutsky fell on the ball and instantly the whole game looked different. Cedarville went into formation for old reliable 33. Mifflin expected a pass because both teams had learned that was the best way to gain yardage in this mud. When the ball was snapped, Mifflin players tried to intercept by rushing toward Bob Harper, whom they saw running around toward the right side of his line. Expecting him to receive, they were caught out of position when Barry passed over his head to Nick Nelson, who had slipped through the enemy line and was in the clear. Bo, also in that territory ready to receive if necessary, now blocked for Nick as he pivoted and headed for the goal line. While Bo stopped one Mifflin back, another reached for Nick just as he bogged down in the mud, struggling valiantly.

Cedarville had gained twenty yards. "We would have made a touchdown if it hadn't been for the mud," one tycoon was heard saying to another. "By Jove, these boys *do* need a better field!"

On the next play, Barry called again for 33. This time an alert Mifflin backfield was laying for both Bo and Nick. Harper also was blocked out of the play. This left Barry without anyone to pass to, so he slipped the ball under his wing and ran around end for a gain of four yards. *Coach was right,* Bo thought. *We can do a lot of different things with this one play.* He wished he could meet the coach and tell him so. Then he had no more time to think about anything except his own job of backing up the line to stop any Mifflin man who broke through.

The half ended with the score still 0–0. Each team retired to its own side of the field. There were no benches, only an old kitchen table and rickety chairs for the score-keeper and timers, one of whom was Mr. Mac with his handy wristwatch. The players sat on the muddy ground, wrapped in faded blankets and ragged quilts brought from home. Katie doled out water, wishing it were hot chocolate. "I wish we had hot dogs too," said Scrubby, busy scraping mud from the team's shoes. When he came to the captain he looked up. "I think you ought to make a touchdown pretty soon, Bo."

"It's a good idea," Bo answered with a grave nod. "Did you hear that, fellows? Scrubby thinks we ought to make a touchdown."

Dick Maull frowned and said to let the kid make one himself if he thought it was so easy. But the others laughed. "Sure we will!" And they pranced onto the field shouting, "Chop! Chop!" when the whistle started the second half.

They soon made their touchdown, on a long pass from Barry to Bo, who carried it over. As he plunged across the dirty white goal line, he felt a deep thrill. Old 33 worked perfectly! Every man did the right thing at exactly the right moment, himself along with the others. *Now we're really playing football!* he thought. When his jubilant teammates gathered round to whack him on the back, he said, "Don't give me the credit! You guys had as much to do with that touchdown as I did." He wasn't trying to sound modest. He meant every word. Barry's accurate pass and the team's well-timed blocking had left him with the easy part. "All I had to do was carry the ball!"

He laughed for joy as he rubbed his hands on his pants and started for the three-yard line for the try for point-after-touchdown. Forgotten now was all the tiresome practice. The only thing that mattered was this tingle in his blood when the play went right. *Man, what a game football is!*

"If you think we'll let you make the point after, you're crazy!" Rodney yelled at him. The Cedarville linemen crouched shoulder to shoulder in stone-wall formation, but a Mifflin end, who had found the weak spot, slipped past Jack Pancake and spoiled the kicker's aim. Losing the point did not even dim Bo's glowing spirits. He made an unexpected discovery. He would rather play good hard football—and lose—then not play at all!

The game went into the last quarter with the 6–0 score still standing. "It looks like you'll be the hero of the game," Katie said to Bo when she brought water during a time-out period. Bo only shook his head and repeated, "It was a team touchdown." He was much more pleased to hear Katie say, "Everybody is talking about what a good game this is. You notice no one is leaving, even though they're standing in mud." She added that she heard several men tell each other these boys were as exciting to watch as many a college team.

The officials broke in with word that the time out was ended. "Five minutes to play!" they informed the captains as the ball was placed.

Both teams were tired now. They did not spring into

formation quite so briskly as in the first quarter. Cedarville had the ball and worked it down to Mifflin's six-yard line.

"Hit 'em again, HARDER!" the home-town crowd shouted over and over. Then came a cheer from the girls, *"Our team is SO sweet!"*

The Mifflin men answered by throwing all their reserve strength into the game. Their greater numbers, size and experience were beginning to tell. Cedarville felt it was trying to batter its way through the Rocky Mountains, yet with dogged courage and persistence it pushed Mifflin back to within five and a half yards of the goal line. There Cedarville lost the ball. As Mifflin prepared to kick out, Bo told his teammates, "If we can block this, we still may make our touchdown."

Then he saw the Mifflin center trying to wipe his eyes. Mud had splattered in the boy's face as the teams sloshed into position, and now he was blinded for a few moments. He was getting in the way of his teammates, who looked around helplessly, not sure what to do. They already had taken the four time-out periods allowed them. Another would cost them a five-yard penalty and bring them back to their own half-yard line—a tricky spot to get out of, where a fumble would mean a sure touchdown for Cedarville.

Mifflin had only a second to make up its mind or else be penalized for delaying the game. Their captain called time out in spite of the penalty. The referee picked up the ball and started to pace off five yards toward the Mifflin goal.

Bo stepped up to the official. "Please bring that ball back to the five-and-a-half yard line," he said. "Cedarville has a time out left. We'll take it now."

"What's the matter with you, Bo?" His teammates were angry. "Don't you want us to make a touchdown?"

"Not that way," Bo answered quietly.

One of Mac's tycoons, an old football player himself no doubt, caught on at once to what had happened. "Bully for you, Cedarville! That's real sportsmanship!" His shout was heard the length of the field.

The Cedarville team now concentrated on making up the yards their captain had lost for them. They rushed the Mifflin kicker, causing the ball to fall short. However, on the next play the slippery ball slid out of Jack Pancake's hands, and immediately a Mifflin player smothered it. Then Mifflin, taking heart, rammed through the weary Cedarville team for three first downs in a row. Next, a couple of chance-taking passes. After all, Mifflin had nothing to lose!

Cedarville was thrown off balance by the suddenness of these tactics. They were trying to pull themselves together when Mifflin whipped a pass over the goal line for a touchdown. Mifflin made the try for the extra point, just as the game ended. Mifflin 7, Cedarville 6.

Bo couldn't believe it. His teammates looked as dazed as he. "We had the game won," they murmured.

"And I threw it away," Bo said quickly, to save them from saying it first. He felt numb. Where was the great glory of the game now? His beaten comrades started from the field without a word, leaving him to follow all alone.

The first person to reach him was one of Mac's tycoons, who tripped over his duck feet in his haste to throw his arms around Bo. "That was the finest act of sportsmanship I ever saw, lad," he said. "We old codgers are grateful to you for keeping up our faith in today's youngsters."

Bo was confused and didn't know how to answer. He saw his father coming toward him with Barry's dad. It was Mr. Bowling who said to the older man, "Bo is my boy, and I'm very proud of him."

Bo was more confused than ever, for he knew Dad and Mr. Hunt both had expected business to keep them away from the game. Now here they were. Barry's dad was smiling and throwing an arm around Barry's shoulders as if the team had won. Bo, thinking the two fathers

188

had just arrived, tried to put them straight at once. "We lost, 7 to 6," he said. "It was my fault."

"What do you mean, your fault?" Barry asked. "Mifflin simply outplayed us the whole last half. If you're thinking of that called-back penalty, Bo, don't blame our defeat on that."

"It helped," Bo said.

"Maybe it did," said Bob Harper, who had dropped back to join Bo. "But we still could have stopped them if we had had the strength. A couple of substitutes would have helped us, for one thing. But that five yards—don't beat yourself about it, Bo. Honestly, we don't blame you for what you did about that penalty."

"Really?" Bo could hardly believe him. The look on his teammates' faces as they gathered around him told him it was true. So they hadn't deliberately turned their backs on him when the game ended! They had only left the field as he himself had—each walking alone in his own defeat and disappointment. Now their crushed spirits were reviving with the good words everyone had to say about their fine sportsmanship. They could hold up their heads again. They looked at one another, beginning to feel the world hadn't come to an end after all. Golly, what a whale of a game it had been!

Bo and Barry suddenly remembered, and rushed to

congratulate Rodney and his team. Victory had put a gleam into Rodney's blank stare but had left his personality unchanged. "I suppose you thought you were going to set a record by winning the Mud Bowl Game," were his first words to Bo. "I told you weeks ago that *I* would teach *you* how to set records."

Bo was saved from having to answer when the *Times* photographer pulled him away, and his mother rushed to hand him a pocket comb and a handkerchief to tidy himself before the picture was snapped. She was too late (to Bo's relief) because the photographer worked very fast. Therefore Bo appeared next Wednesday on the front page of the *Two-Village Times* with torn pants, mud-smeared face, and hair standing on end.

"Look, dear! The editor has even written an editorial about you," she said, after she had cried over and admired the picture.

"Is that it?" Bo, looking over her shoulder, pointed beneath his picture to the extra wide column of type. It was headed, "A Salute to Fine Sportsmanship" and was signed: The Editor. It was all about a boy who did what Bo had done in the Mud Bowl Game, and how he was "an example of the high type of boy developed by football and other sports." *He must mean me,* Bo thought. This was hard to believe, because that other boy—the one in type—did not seem real. Neither could he believe his teammates were the ones referred to as "these excellent junior citizens in our community who have shown so plainly where character is built and who have put the question squarely up to Cedarville: Why don't we have a playing field?"

Bo was the town hero for the rest of the week—until State U. played its last game of the season and Scott Freeman ended as the leading touchdown scorer in the nation. The news wasn't certain until all other college games had been played and the scores checked. It was Sunday afternoon before a sportscaster for one of the big city papers gave the definite announcement on radio that Freeman of Cedarville had made twenty-two touchdowns during the season, which was more than any other college player in the country had made.

When Bo heard this, he was out of the house with a whoop, and across the street to tell Barry. Soon those two and Katie started out to spread the good news wherever it was not already known, for they knew all Cedarville was hoping its favorite son would prove himself the Number 1 Touchdown Maker.

"We must tell Scrubby first," Katie said. The boys said Scrubby could find out later. They had to hurry to tell their teammates. As they rushed off, Scrubby must have seen them, for out he came—"What you *doo-oo*-ing?"— and tagged along. Other boys joined them until finally there was a regular snake dance winding down the street and through the business section, past Shinkledecker's, past Muzzey's Laundromat and Squeeo the Plumber, to Ryan's Pharmacy. There the procession entered, each youngster with a hand on the shoulder of the one ahead of him, and all shouting, " 'Ray for Scotty *Free*-man, leader of the *Nay*-shun." The chain wound around the showcases and out the door again.

Tom Ryan stood with his hands in the pockets of his white coat, laughing and cheering. His customers at first looked startled, then began to cheer as hard as the boys and girls. They all agreed with Tom, who said, wiping tears of laughter from his eyes as the cheering died away in the distance, "Yes, sir, that's a mighty fine bunch of boys and girls. Our town is lucky to have 'em."

On went the snake dance led by Bo and Barry, who now steered toward Mr. Mac's shop. "Do you think he'll be there? It's Sunday," Barry reminded Bo above the din. Bo, being too hoarse by this time to speak, simply nodded. He knew Mac was so fond of inventing he couldn't stay away from his work even on Sunday afternoons. As they came in sight of Nantaquas, Mac himself stepped out as if to see what the shouting was about.

"Did you hear about Scotty?" Barry yelled. Mac nodded and jig-stepped and threw one arm around Nantaquas to show how much the news pleased him. "I talked to the editor on the phone just now," he said, although nobody could hear him except Bo, who was standing at his side. "He is already working on a civic celebration for Scott."

The *Times* that week told all about the affair. It was to be a big banquet at the Cedarville-Mifflin Community Church, backed by the Boosters Club and cooked by the Ladies Aid. Since Scotty had grown up very near the boundary line between the two villages, Mifflin citizens claimed a share in his fame, and were buying almost as many tickets to the dinner in his honor as Cedarville folks were. Finally word went out that all the tickets were gone. Bo and his parents had bought theirs, and so had the Hunts, but what about Bo's other teammates? He was afraid some of them would have to miss the banquet, when—of all people!—Rodney Sanders solved the problem. He phoned with a message from his mother. She belonged to the Ladies Aid of the Community Church, which was putting on the dinner. Since the church had as many members from Cedarville as from Mifflin, she had the delightful idea of asking the high school teams and some of the younger players in both places to act as waiters at the dinner for the gridiron hero. Bo, of course, accepted at once for himself and all his teammates. He then gave his ticket to Scrubby, who may have been too young to understand banquet speech making, but who certainly had done his bit for football in the community that season.

More and more national honors were heaped on Scott Freeman. He was named on everybody's All-American team. He was given cups and watches and medals. He appeared on TV programs and became known from coast to coast as Mr. Football. Cedarville, wanting the greatest award of all to come from his own home town, decided to give him an automobile. When Scott heard of the plan he immediately telephoned the *Two-Village Times.* "And he put a stop to it," the editor told Bo, whom he met in Ryan's drugstore. "Scotty was very nice about it, but he said he wouldn't feel right about taking a car from us. He said he hadn't done anything to deserve it. You know how modest he is, Tom—" the editor turned to Mr. Ryan, who was behind the counter.

The druggist said, "Yes, sir—but did you tell him people already have donated enough money for the car?"

"He said if we couldn't give the money back, he hoped we would use it for the kids' play field." With a pleased smile the editor confessed, "I'm very glad he did that.

You see, thanks to this boy here—" he tapped Bo's shoulder, "—I had already started a little campaign for a field fund. Then Scotty shot into the national headlines and everybody forgot these youngsters and their valiant Mud Bowl efforts. The *Times* had to go along with public sentiment, naturally. So my newspaper—and you Boosters of course—raised the money to buy him a car. But I couldn't help wishing the money were going for the kids' football field. Now, they'll get it after all!"

"And Scott Freeman has shown that his sportsmanship is as great off the gridiron as on it," Tom Ryan said.

"How did Scotty find out? About the car, I mean," Bo asked. In spite of the way things had turned out, he was disappointed that Scotty would not have the car. It was to have been a secret, and he had been looking forward to seeing Scotty's surprise. "How do you suppose he ever found out?" he asked again.

"Maybe Coach Teneyes told him," Tom Ryan said with a sly look.

"Who *is* that guy?" the editor demanded.

"Maybe you'll get to meet him at the banquet," the druggist said, moving off to wait on a customer.

"Is *he* coming to the banquet?" Bo couldn't help calling out. Tom shrugged and kept on going. Bo was in such a lather of excitement he didn't see how he could last until the big night. He had counted on seeing Scotty then. Imagine meeting Coach Teneyes too! He hoped the boys who served wouldn't be kept in the back of the dining room. He wanted to be close enough to the speakers' table to get a good look at everyone seated there.

CHAPTER FOURTEEN

Rodney's Last Remark

Bo need not have worried about being close to the Very Important Persons at the banquet. On the evening of the dinner, just as he was shining his shoes, the editor telephoned to say Bo was expected to sit at the speakers' table. "Me? At the seekers' stable?" Bo was overcome by excitement.

"We thought you ought to be there with the honored guests," the editor said calmly. "As captain of the Cedarville team."

Bo was in control of himself now. He said he'd sit there as soon as he finished helping wait on the tables and had his own dinner.

"Forget about serving!" The editor said Bo was to sit in the place of honor for dinner, for the program, for the whole affair.

Golly day!

After Bo told his mother, she said he'd better go upstairs and change to his new suit. "Your second best one was good enough as long as you were serving and might have spilled something on it, but now—" she broke off to say, "I must call Lila Sanders right away and tell her the banquet committee will be minus one waiter tonight."

"Minus *two* waiters," Bo called down the steps. "Rodney's a team captain too, so he'll be sitting with me." Any other time Bo would have frowned at the thought of being with Rodney for an evening. Now he was glad to have another boy to keep him company.

However, when he arrived at the church vestibule, where he had been told to come, he saw no sign of Rodney. "Here's our young captain," the editor said, coming forward to shake his hand and to introduce him to a group of men standing around. One of them was Mr. Mac, neatly pressed and combed. Bo almost didn't recognize him without a streak of grease on his face. Several of the other men Bo remembered seeing at the Mud Bowl Game. They were Mac's friends, whom he called the tycoons. They were talking in dollars. So many hundreds for drainage tile. So many more for dirt fill, and for grading and for grass seed. Bo did not realize these were things needed in making a good football field. The conversation

198

bored him. Instead of listening he looked for a way to escape downstairs to the dining room to be with the other boys. He knew at this time they would be filling water glasses on the long tables, where football fans of the two villages were beginning to seat themselves.

Then the door opened and in came Scott Freeman like the sun lighting up the world on a cloudy day. At once Bo felt happy and contented. The men smiled and hooray-ed. As they shoved forward, eager as boys to touch the hero's hand, Bo was blocked out of sight. Scotty saw him, though, and reached past the bald heads to clap him on the shoulder. "It's great to see you again, Bo!"

Scotty remembered him! Bo tried to stammer his congratulations on Mr. Football's honors. At the same time Scotty was saying, "We did a good job that Sunday we started a team, didn't we? I hear you really took care of football in Cedarville this fall."

"It was all on account of that play you showed us," Bo said. "We wouldn't even have been a team without that. We practiced and practiced it. Coach Teneyes told us— say, Scotty, do you know him?"

Scott grinned. He said he didn't suppose he knew him any better than Bo did. He added, "He is going to be here tonight, they tell me."

Bo took his eyes off Scotty long enough to look around

the room. He knew none of the men he had been introduced to was named Teneyes. He wondered about the three or four who had come in late. There was not time to find out about them because the editor now was hopping from guest to guest with a list of names, saying, "It's time for us to go in. I'll line you up according to the way you'll find your places at the speakers' table. And I want you to stay put."

Bo gave up hope of being seated next to Scotty when he heard the editor say, "Mr. Football, you're to sit between your old high school principal and yours truly, the toastmaster." Bo was placed next in line, beside Mr. Mac. He was glad for that.

The line began to move downstairs into the dining room. Bo, who had kept on the watch for Rodney, now gave up. He decided he alone had been chosen for this honor because he captained the team Scott Freeman had started. "Oh, boy!" he said to himself. "This is great! Me at the speakers' table and old Rodney passing the soup! I can hardly wait to see the look on his face."

He soon saw it. But it was no different than usual. Rodney stared straight through him as if Bo weren't there.

Then Bo forgot everything else and floated off in a bubble of candlelight on a sea of murmuring voices. One of the voices became more distinct. "Eat your soup," said Mr. Mac.

Bo tasted. It was his favorite, split pea soup. "Oh!" he sputtered in excitement. "Slit sea poup! Yum yum."

By the time the soup plates were taken away, he was feeling more at home in the public gaze. Looking around, he saw his mother and dad at a table down in front. He hoped no one noticed the little secret signal Mother made to show she was throwing him a kiss. He gave her a quick nod, then turned his attention to the decorations on the speakers' table. The centerpiece was the famous bronze football. He wondered whose name would be engraved upon it from among Cedarville's players of this season. He looked over the high school team members now serving plates of chicken and mashed potatoes. He tried to decide which boy might be the one whose name was to be announced later in the evening.

As the meal came to an end, the editor rose to speak about what he called the true meaning of football. "Some people," he began with a quick glance at a small card in his hand, "think football is nothing more than a game. Only a game—in which small boys shove one another around, tear up the lawn and forget to come in to supper. Only a game—in which young fellows run with, throw, or push an odd-shaped ball across a white line painted on the grass, while a lot of old fellows like me cheer for them . . . This is not what football is at all.

"Football is really a school. On the football field boys study the most important lesson they have to learn. The lesson on how to become a man . . . A man strong in body. A man who is honest, and who will never cheat to win. A man who will stand squarely with his comrades in battle, yet can treat a hard-pressed enemy with noble unselfishness . . . A man who can fight down the fear inside himself—" here Bo understood what the editor was talking about as he remembered the shaky feeling he always had before a game.

"Football players who fail to learn these gridiron lessons, do not deserve to be called team men at all. Those who do learn them, teach us ordinary folk how important such schooling is," the editor went on. "Scott Freeman has taught our whole nation a lesson in what a fine man should be."

Everybody started clapping, until Scotty had to rise and take a bow to quiet them so the editor could continue. "Scotty has indeed been well named *Mr. Football*. We are proud, too, that growing up here and following in his footsteps, we have a *young* Mr. Football . . . A couple of weeks ago, in a game played in ankle-deep mud and ending with defeat for his team, this lad taught us that good sportsmanship counts more than a high score. He proved to us that there are defeats more triumphant than victories . . ." The words rolled over Bo's head until he caught a familiar sound—". . . name is Harold Bowling . . . Bo, suppose you stand up so everybody can see you."

Bo was so surprised he couldn't move. "Get up! Get up!" Mac whispered, pushing back his chair for him. Bo rose. *Golly, what a lot of people were looking at him. And clapping!* He sat down at once. The people laughed and clapped harder. The editor stopped them with a wave of his hand and went on, "Bo also showed us that sports-loving boys are very valuable to our community. In return we owe them the right sort of place in which to play their games and learn their lessons in manhood . . . But there are others here who have something to say along these lines. I shall now call upon them."

Speakers rose in turn to pay honor to Scotty or to talk about money already raised and money still needed for the recreation field. Pledge cards were passed to the audience to be filled out and signed. Bo paid small attention to all this. He long ago had decided grown-ups often have a lot more to say than he could listen to. Therefore he occupied himself now with locating his teammates in various parts of the room and in exchanging smiles with Katie, Scrubby and his teacher, whom he was pleased to see there. Rodney of course ignored him.

When Scott Freeman began to speak, however, Bo came to attention. Scotty thanked his townspeople and friends for their cheers during the football season and for this fine banquet in his honor, as well as for the automobile they had tried to give him. Then he asked for a round of applause for all the younger athletes in the audience. "By the way," he said when the clapping died away, "I have been asked to introduce the coach of our Cedarville boys' team. He is known as Coach Teneyes."

The speaker paused. Bo's eyes darted into every corner, looking for a man rising to his feet. No one stirred. Scotty went on, "This rather mysterious coach of our famous Mud Bowl team is himself a good example of what the toastmaster tonight calls the true meaning of football . . . In the first place, let me explain that Coach Teneyes is not one man, but five—as you may have guessed from his name."

"Of course! Why didn't I think of that?" Bo asked himself. "I wonder who the five are."

"Three of them played football in their college days. So when the boys wanted a coach, each of these men offered to do the job. For love of the game they would have been glad to give time and energy to pass along to young players the most important lessons of football. But the boys turned down each one of them. Then the kids wanted me for their coach. But, as you know, I was kind of busy this fall." There were chuckles from the audience although Scotty was serious as he went on. "I wanted to help because I hated to see a bunch of kids learn their first steps in football the wrong way, or perhaps give up the game entirely, for lack of proper coaching. Those other three men, unbeknown to me or to one another, felt the same as I did. It took Man Number 5 to bring us all together. He understands what football can mean to boys, although he never played it. He is an inventor."

"You!" Bo turned to Mr. Mac, who only smiled.

"This inventor," Scotty was saying, "on a dare from some of the youngsters, promised he would invent them a coach. The kids had already told him about me and about those other three fellows, so he put us together and made a coach, by gum! He intended to keep himself out of it. The four of us who knew football were to divide the work of sending messages of instruction to the team and of watching the kids practice whenever we could. But we found we needed somebody to carry the messages. So, as our inventor agreed, five heads were better than four, and ten eyes were better than eight."

Bo was about to whisper to Mac, "Why did you keep it a secret?" when Scotty gave the answer.

"We deliberately made Coach Teneyes a mystery because grown-up boys enjoy making fun for younger ones. Besides—" he grinned, "—the three of us who had been brushed aside unwanted, felt the team would lose confidence if it learned they were in on the deal . . . As you must have guessed by now, Coach Teneyes is another of the successful inventions of Mr. T. Edison MacGillicuddy . . . Save your applause, please, until I have finished the introductions, when Coach Teneyes will stand in a body. Or rather, in five bodies."

Murmurs of surprise were heard as he spoke the names. "In addition to Mac and me, there are Tom Ryan . . . Bill Hunt . . . (*Barry's father!* Bo felt his mouth drop open with amazement.) . . . and a newcomer to Cedarville, whom some of you older sports fans used to read about as Nebraska's great fullback, Hal Bowling."

Bo was dumbfounded. Beside him he felt Mac get to his feet. Out in the crowd he saw Tom Ryan and Mr. Hunt rise. Then his own father stood up and smiled at him while cheers and applause swept over the tables. *What a good joke on me!* Bo thought. *My own father, and I never even suspected.* He laughed and clapped harder than anybody.

The editor rose, confessed he also never had suspected the identity of Coach Teneyes, and asked the high school cheer leaders to do their stuff. "First, though—" he took a quick look at his notes,"—Jim Bidwell, captain of the high school team, will go among you, collecting those cards upon which I hope you have written a generous pledge to the Mud Bowl Playing Field Fund."

Bo never had seen Jim Bidwell before. Now as he admired the tall boy with the firm jaw and husky shoulders, he said to himself, "I'll bet he's the one whose name will be put on the football trophy. He looks like a wonderful fellow."

While the cheers died away, the editor rapped on the table to bring everyone back to business. "The final feature of this delightful evening is the announcement of the new name to be engraved on the Cedarville football trophy. But before we come to that—" he glanced at his notes again, "—I'd like to say that some of our brains here at the speakers' table have already totaled the amounts you good people have pledged. This sum, added to the cash already raised, makes a grand total sufficient to turn the old Mud Bowl into the finest football field boys ever had. There will be tennis courts too—" Bo was sure he heard a whoop of joy from Katie, "—because our girls are just as important to us as our boys, and we want them both to have the same opportunities for fun and physical training.

"And now—" he stuck his cards in a baggy pocket and laid one hand on the gleaming bronze football in front of him, "—who else could we possibly select as the boy who has done the most this season to carry on the football tradition in Cedarville? Who else but the one whose high sportsmanship and love of the game caused our town to open its eyes and its pocketbooks to the need of our boys and girls for something better than a Mud Bowl? The Boosters Club was unanimous in voting to engrave upon this trophy, where it will stand for years to come, to inspire Cedarville boys—the name of Harold Bowling."

The words roared in Bo's ears. *Stand for years to come . . . the name of Harold Bowling . . . will stand for years to come.*

"Me?" He couldn't believe it. He looked at Mac, who was beaming at him and pounding the table. Mac pushed him to his feet as the applause thundered over him. It was Mac who whispered presently, "You can sit down now." Bo wasn't able to think of anything except that he was sure there had been a mistake. He turned to Mac. "I mink they thent the high cool scaptain, instead of me. He—he's a real player. I'm just—just—"

"You're just the kid who started from scratch, without

a team or a coach or a place to play," Mac said, shaking his hand. "And now see what happened because you were willing to dig in and help yourself along!"

The banquet was over. People crowded to the long table to talk to Scott Freeman. Many of them came to tell Bo they were proud of "young Mr. Football" too. His dad and mother stood in the background looking very happy. With them were Aunt Lila and Uncle Harry Sanders and Rodney. When Bo was free to join them, they all said nice things about his honor. Even Rodney, whose manners as always were excellent in front of grownups, managed smooth congratulations. However, as he stared at the football he added, "Too bad it is merely bronze, Bo. Mifflin is going to get a trophy—I expect to set a record so my name will be the first one on it—and it is going to be *gold*."

Bo answered oh, so quietly, "Let me know when you set a record." Weeks ago Rodney had taunted him with these very same words. Now Rodney knew about the record Bo had set. So did everybody else in the two villages.

"And everyone around here will remember you forever!" Katie said a little later as she and he and Barry were saying goodnight under the big tree in Bo's yard. All three were still too excited to feel sleepy, so they warmed their hands in their pockets and tapped their chilly toes on the cold ground, and went on talking until their parents called.

For the first time Bo realized he didn't have to worry any more about moving away and being forgotten. No matter where he went, he would have friends back in Cedarville. He heard Barry say, "You sure made a name for yourself here. Yippee-yeaaaa, Bo!" Barry's cheer rang on the cold night air.

From an open bedroom window of the house next door came a familiar cry. "What you *doo-oo*-ing?"

Katie called out, "Scrubby, why aren't you asleep?"

"I want to see the football that's got Bo's name on it," Scrubby shouted back.

"Pipe down and go to sleep," Barry told him. "You'll see it someday."

So he will, Bo thought. Someday when Scrubby was old enough to read, he would see the bronze football in the library. By then Bo would be playing on another team in some far distant town. Now he smiled to himself in the dark as he thought of Scrubby at that time, standing in front of the trophy and pointing to a certain name. "I know him," Scrubby would tell the other boys. "He lived next door to me when I was little."

RUBRICS

Peel off...

The...

Manufactured Cards